DARK HILLS TO WESTWARD

The Saga of Jenny Wiley

DARK HILLS TO WESTWARD

The Saga of Jenny Wiley

by
Harry M. Caudill

with an Epilogue by
Anne F. Caudill

illustrated by
Jim Marsh

The Jesse Stuart Foundation
Ashland, Kentucky
1994

Dark Hills to Westward:
The Saga of Jenny Wiley

Library of Congress Cataloging-in-Publication Data

Caudill, Harry M., 1922-
    Dark hills to westward : the saga of Jenny Wiley / by Harry M.
Caudill : with an epilogue by Anne F. Caudill.
        p. cm.
    ISBN 0-945084-45-5
    1. Wiley, Jennie Sellards, d. 1831--Fiction. 2. Frontier and
pioneer life--Kentucky--Fiction. 3. Indian captivities--Kentucky-
-Fiction. 4. Women pioneers--Kentucky--Fiction. I. Title.
PS3553.A9D37 1994
813'.54--dc20   94-19890
                                                                CIP

Published by:
The Jesse Stuart Foundation
P.O. Box 391
Ashland, KY 41114
1997

For Wendell Berry --
After my wife my favorite Kentuckian

EDITOR'S PREFACE

Kentucky's pioneer history has proved fertile ground for writers of literature as well as for historians. Nineteenth-century writers of historical fiction like John Alexander McClung, Robert Montgomery Bird, and James Weir paved the way for twentieth century novelists like Joseph Alexander Altsheler, Janice Holt Giles, and Elizabeth Maddox Roberts.

In *The Great Meadow*, perhaps the best novel ever written on Kentucky frontier life, Roberts describes the opening of the land beyond the Appalachian mountains as an American epic, observing of Daniel Boone and his contemporaries that "there were giants in the earth in those days." The same might be said of the generation of authors that followed her onto the dark and bloody ground of Kentucky's frontier fiction. Certainly one of those giants was the late Harry M. Caudill, a highly respected statesman and, at times, a controversial polemicist.

Best known for non-fiction works like *Night Comes to the Cumberlands* and *The Watches of the Night*, Caudill also wrote fiction, including *Dark Hills to Westward: The Saga of Jenny Wiley*, first published in 1969. A preacher sat down with Jenny Wiley in 1831 and wrote out her story, and although Jenny may have embellished it many times, it is the only first-hand account we have.

It is also the basis for Caudill's novel. He traces Jenny's year in captivity—a time when she saw her babies murdered and a white captive tortured to death—and tells the thrilling story of her escape. It is not a story for young children or the faint of heart! His vivid prose presents a clear picture of Jenny's courage, and offers keen insight into the physical fatigue and psychological stress of her ordeal. As the late William S. Ward observed in *A Literary History of Kentucky*, Caudill does more than tell Jenny Wiley's story: "He achieves a picture of a time and place in history when toughness, courage, and resourcefulness were essential human qualities if one were to survive." Jenny was a survivor.

Briefly, this is Jenny's story: Thomas and Jenny Wiley had pioneered land on Walker's Creek in Bland County, Virginia. On October 1, 1789, while Thomas was away, a small band of Indians, seeking revenge for a recent defeat at the hands of white settlers, attacked the Wiley cabin and killed and scalped Jenny's three older children and her brother. Jenny, seven months pregnant, was taken captive along with her baby son, Adam.

Then began a nightmare flight through the wilderness into the dark Kentucky hills to westward. Jenny's only hope for survival was to keep pace with her captors. On the third day, a Cherokee Chief snatched the sick child from its horrified mother and smashed little Adam Wiley's brains out against a tree. Evading rescue parties, the Indians moved northwest into the Big Sandy Valley of Kentucky. Unable to cross the flood-swollen Ohio River, they retreated to a series of winter camps in present-day Carter, Lawrence, and Johnson counties.

With only a rock bluff for shelter, Jenny spent the winter laboring as a slave. She gave birth in a cave, but three months later the Indians killed and scalped the infant, after it failed to pass their test of courage. After almost a year in captivity, Jenny escaped, miraculously evading pursuit as she made her way to a small settlement at Harman's Station on John's Creek. Readers will thrill to the story of her escape and return to her husband.

Immediately upon its publication in 1969, *The Saga of Jenny Wiley* was hailed as a significant contribution to the body of literature and lore that surrounds this frontier heroine. Among the kindred studies useful for background information are *Jenny Wiley, Pioneer Mother and Borderland Heroine* by Henry P. Scalf of Prestonsburg, and *The Founding of Harman's Station and the Wiley Captivity* by William Elsey Connelley, with four additional chapters by Edward R. Hazelett of Paintsville.

When Caudill published *Jenny Wiley*, he was already nationally known as the author of *Night Comes to the Cumberlands*, a study of Appalachian poverty which had burst upon the national scene six years earlier. This book brought Caudill a well-deserved national reputation as a spokesman for Appalachia and he was seen as an expert on the region's economic and social problems. This reputation prompted immediate interest in his novel, which was widely reviewed.

While the reviewers praised *Jenny Wiley*, they also found fault with Caudill's venture into historical fiction. The book received criticism for poor character development and unconvincing dialogue, but the harshest criticisms concerned Caudill's treatment of the Indians as simply bloodthirsty savages. Tom Bethell's detailed and

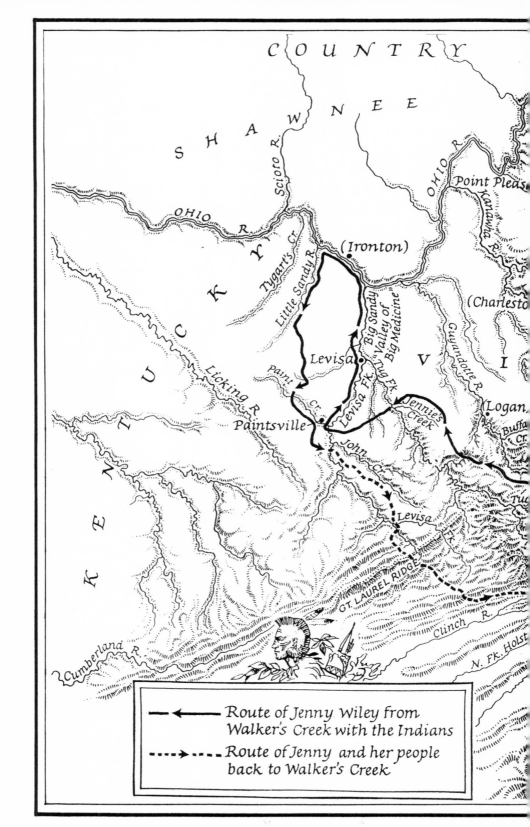

C O U N T R Y

S H A W N E E

Scioro R.

OHIO R.

Tygart's Cr.

Little Sandy R.

(Ironton)

Big Sandy "Valley of
Big Medicine"

Levisa

Levisa Fk.

Right Fk.

Paint Cr.

Licking R.

Paintsville

John Cr.

Jennies Creek

K E N T U C K Y

Levisa Fk.

GT. LAUREL RIDGE

Clinch R.

Cumberland R.

N. Fk. Holst

Point Pleas

Kanawha R.

OHIO R.

(Charlesto

Guyandotte R.

V I

(Logan,

Buffa Cr.

Tu

— ←	Route of Jenny Wiley from Walker's Creek with the Indians
····►····	Route of Jenny and her people back to Walker's Creek

Dark Hills to Westward

Scale of Miles

0 5 10   20   30   40   50   60

insightful review in *The Mountain Eagle* (Whitesburg, Kentucky) offered a middle-ground assessment: "The treatment of Indians weakens this book; but it is still a first-rate piece of storytelling—occasionally in a class with Mark Twain and Kenneth Roberts and always unraveled with the kind of persistent enthusiasm that makes Harry Caudill well worth listening to, and well worth reading."

So, be forewarned. If you are looking for a "politically correct" version of race relations, you will not find it here. Like the great fireside storytellers that Harry M. Caudill descended from and represented, he tells a searing story from the perspective of Jenny and her white contemporaries. Readers should keep in mind that Caudill did not write the book as an historian, but as a storyteller, and his goal was to tell Jenny's story as she experienced it.

Several changes have been made in the 1997 edition of *The Saga of Jenny Wiley*. The book has been completely redesigned, with larger page size and print size for easier reading. A lengthy historical Introduction has been moved to the end of the text and re-titled "Author's Historical Afterword." The spelling of "Jennie" has been changed to "Jenny" to conform to general usage, and there are some other stylistic modifications. At the request of his widow, Anne F. Caudill, the text of the book stands as Harry Caudill wrote it more than twenty-five years ago.

The 1997 edition has been enhanced by Anne Caudill's Epilogue, which provides background information on the research and writing of *Jenny Wiley*. It also includes Mrs. Caudill's personal insights into her late husband's life and accomplishments. The Jesse Stuart Foundation gratefully acknowledges the kindness of *Appalachian Heritage* in allowing us to reprint a portion of this essay, originally published in the Spring 1993 issue under the title "Life with a Polemicist."

Dark Hills to Westward: The Saga of Jenny Wiley would be useful in college-level courses that deal with Women's History or Appalachian History, or it would be an excellent supplementary text in American History survey courses. It is a must for adult readers who want to learn more about pioneer life in Eastern Kentucky and Southern Appalachia.

The Jesse Stuart Foundation is proud to add the name of Harry M. Caudill to a distinguished list of JSF authors that includes Jesse Stuart, Billy C. Clark, Loyal Jones, Thomas D. Clark, James B. Goode, and many others.

James M. Gifford

Harry M. Caudill 1922 to 1990

INTRODUCTION

Many versions of the Jenny Wiley legend have survived in eastern Kentucky and southwestern Virginia, and they differ from one another in many respects. Jenny and most of her frontier contemporaries were illiterate and those who could write seldom did so. The earliest accounts of her story were written down nearly eighty years after her death. The oral transmissions have doubtless brought down to us embellishments and modifications—the results of active imaginations in fireside storytellers.

Even the year of her abduction is in doubt. Varying traditions relate that she was carried into captivity in 1779, in 1787, or in 1789. According to one line of Jenny's descendants, her maiden name was Stallard rather than Sellards. There is dispute about the location of the Wiley farm—was it on Walker's Creek or in Ab's Valley? Another legend has it that some of her children survived the massacre and were carried away to Ohio.

Thus some of the traditional details recorded in these pages may be in error. We can never know for certain, but they make up the story as I believe it occurred. Some parts of the legend have been omitted as wholly improbable or even impossible. It must be conceded, however, that on the frontier the unthinkable often happened, and it is possible that in the exercise of what I have deemed a reasonable judgement Jenny and her story have been caused to suffer.

Sometimes, too, the storytellers fall silent, leaving intriguing voids only the imagination can fill. Sometimes credence must be given to strange sources if continuity is to survive at all. For example, I am indebted to a bearded, somewhat tipsy octogenarian for history of the battle at the cliff when the Indians attempted to recapture the white squaw. He swore: "Afore God, that's the way I have always heerd it told."

In any event, Jenny Wiley lived and toiled, suffered and died. In the nation's great epic struggle she was one of many unsung heroines. Of the central thread of her story there can be no doubt. If she and some of the characters who touched her life can live again in the reader's mind, I will be pleased. Such people should not be forgotten.

Harry M. Caudill
February 14, 1969

CHAPTER ONE

Long before it was safe to do so—perhaps as early as 1760—Hezekiah Sellards led a dozen families out of the Shenandoah Valley into the wilds of western Virginia. They settled on Walker's Creek near the foot of Walker's Mountain, in what is now Bland County. They brought with them herds of sheep, cattle and hogs, flocks of chickens and packs of vicious dogs. They brought, also, a detestation of the Indians upon whose ancient hunting grounds they insolently built their cabins, and a steadfast resolve to hold their new settlement however high the cost in blood and agony.

Sellards was Scotch-Irish and his Presbyterianism bordered on fanaticism. He had the strength and undoubting determination of an Old Testament prophet. His two sons, Thomas and Jack, and his daughters, Jenny and Elizabeth, were taught from the cradle the virtues of cleanliness, courage, diligence and toil. Since he was a man of few utterances, he taught by example, and the harsh backwoods environment emphasized his precepts. Under his leadership and guidance the isolated little community withstood Indian forays—some of them in impressive strength—for a whole generation.

By 1789 Sellards was infirm with old age and his mantle of leadership had descended to a younger man, a "Dutchman" named Matthias Harman. "Tice" Harman was a caricature of a frontiersman. He was five feet tall and weighed no more than a hundred and twenty pounds, "sopping wet." His thin face was hidden by a curly yellow beard, and his small blue eyes were so pale as to be nearly colorless. His enormous Roman nose swept far outward and descended to a point almost in front of his broad mouth with its rows of sturdy teeth. He carried a huge butcher knife in a scabbard at his belt and his .46-caliber Pennsylvania rifle was taller than he. Unlike the calm and dignified Sellards, he was a man with a fearless temper.

Despite his comical appearance, he was a thoroughly serious figure on the frontier. A splendid athlete, he had spent his life prowling through the western wilderness. He had fought Indians since he was twelve or thirteen years old and was feared and respected by a half-dozen tribes. To the Shawnee he was known as "Ski-goos-tee-ay"—"the Little Devil with a Big Nose."

He was a resourceful and cunning backwoodsman, and all his strength and skill were needed to defend and extend the little settlement.

In 1789 settlements were growing rapidly in the Kentucky Bluegrass, but it would be five years before the battle of Fallen Timbers would shatter the power of the Indians in Ohio and the Northwest and a half-dozen years after that before the Cherokee grip on the southern end of the range would be broken. The Cherokee, Wyandot, Choctaw, Mingo, Shawnee and Delaware—virtually all the region's Indian tribes—had sided with the English during the Revolution and the whole frontier had flamed. The aborigines had sensed that they could make some sort of tolerable arrangement with Britain, but they knew without doubt that if the revolutionaries prevailed they would stand cheek to jowl with destruction at the hands of the land-hungry backwoodsmen of the Piedmont and Shenandoah. With the Revolution, Indian power in the Alleghenies and Appalachians drew near its end. Undermined by the withdrawal of the English and by a growing dependence on trade goods, and outraged by the bold and insatiable demands of the backwoodsmen for their lands, the tribes were demoralized and chaotic. Fragments of tribes still held out throughout the range, but in the main they had moved into the low hills north of the Ohio and into the towering mountains of the Tennessee territory. From there they struck out in bloody raids against the settlements. A much-used war trail crossed the Ohio near the present site of Ironton, wound up the Big Sandy Valley to the forks of the river, then followed the Tug Fork through the Great Laurel (sometimes called the Big Sandy) Ridge. Threading through gaps in the numerous long ridges that wrinkle the central Appalachians, the "trace" led into the fastnesses of the majestic Great Smokies. This dim trail was a tie binding the Shawnee and other northern people to their southern brethren. Similar trails followed the Kanawha and Bluestone. Any man courageous enough to build a cabin within reach of the war parties that used these wilderness roads courted a hideous death.

The Appalachians were a gigantic forest. Magnificent trees covered the narrow river bottoms and clothed the steeply sloping hills. Black loam a foot or more thick carpeted the forest floor. Where fire had cleared patches of bottom land there were canebrakes tangled almost to impenetrability. In a few areas squaws had deadened timber and planted fields of corn. The long hunters knew such plots as "Indian Old Fields." The Hill Cherokee, particularly, had inhabited these mountains for centuries and loved them with a passion.

The vast forest teemed with wildlife. There were enough bison to leave behind such names as Buffalo Creek and Bull Lick. Black bear, deer, elk, mountain lions, bobcats, squirrels and birds abounded. The mountains were a hunter's paradise, and Harman and his settlers loved to hunt. Not many of them would ever amount to much as farmers, but they saw scant need to farm in a land where every stream fluttered with fish and hillsides rustled with game.

At Walker's Creek a little blockhouse was built in a clearing. All stumps within rifle range were burned off level with the ground. Loopholes were cut at strategic points and the fort was fitted with a massive oak door. It was provisioned with enough water, parched corn and smoked meat to support forty or fifty people for a week. The station was a refuge to be sought only as a matter of last resort. The people in their little cabins depended on their woodcraft to detect Indians before they could strike and on one another to sound the alarm in time to band together to repel attacks.

The settlement was of diverse origins. The oldest member was born Heinrich Herrmann in Prussia eighty-six years before. Now called Henry Harman, he had three sons in the settlement in addition to Tice—George, Henry and Daniel. Originally they had come out of the Shenandoah with four other "Dutchmen"—Casper Mansker and Michael Holsteiner, the latter known simply Mike Stoner, and the Skaggs brothers, Henry and James. These Germans were superlative backwoodsmen and Indian fighters and scouted much of the western border, often beating trails for their redoubtable Scotch, Irish and English compatriots. In 1789 Henry Skaggs was seventy-five but had the bearing and strength of a man twenty years younger.

John Borders was an Englishman who had come to America as a British soldier soon after the outbreak of the Revolution. Captured with Cornwallis at Yorktown, he remained several months in prison and when paroled moved to the Virginia backwoods. He was a tall man with strong, heavy hands, courageous black eyes and a large reservoir of steady courage. He married Elizabeth Sellards.

In 1778, when she was eighteen, Hezekiah Sellards's other daughter, Jenny, married Thomas Wiley, a young immigrant from Northern Ireland. Six months after landing in Maryland he had followed the trading trails to the backwoods and attached himself to Tice Harman.

Neither Wiley nor Borders ever became a highly skilled woodsman. Brave and intelligent though they were, they remained Europeans by instinct. Despite a willingness to learn, many of the subtle nuances of woodcraft escaped them and they remained insensitive to much that their backwoods friends knew almost subconsciously.

A year or two after Thomas arrived his brother, Samuel, joined the settlement. Three other young men named Robert Hawes, George Draper and Lazarus Damron visited the valley on a hunting expedition and returned with their wives and children. Later Absalom Lusk built a cabin in Ab's Valley not far from Samuel Wiley's. These men and their families were probably America's western-most outpost within the immense mountain territory lying between the Tennessee and Ohio rivers. At unpredictable intervals they were visited by solitary hunters named Holbrook, Fraley, Cowen or Logan, and sometimes by friendly Indians bent on trade.

The Sellards sisters were the kind of women men have admired in every setting. Jenny, especially, was remarkable. She was a large woman, not beautiful perhaps, but handsome and magnetic, with a streak of auburn in her coal-black hair. Her forehead was high and broad and her jet eyes were arched with brows a little too heavy for perfection. They were quick and searching with a trace of good humor sparkling in their depths. Her nose was strong and prominently arched, but not too large. Her gleaming white teeth and strong supple hands reflected good health and quick strength.

She had a steady competence, as befitted a daughter of Hezekiah Sellards. She liked to weave and her loom produced the linsey-woolsey that clothed her husband and children. She was a gardener and grew in the forest loam many vegetables unknown to other backwoods tables. And she was courageous. Harman admired her as a better shot and a steadier hand than most men.

Jenny had known the shadows of the great forest since birth. She had never lived for a moment beyond reach of marauding Indians. When as a child she ventured into the forest she carried the warnings of her elders in her ears: "Watch and listen for Indians! The redskins may be anywhere!"

Consequently, her eyes and ears never rested. When she and her husband worked about their cabin or when he labored in a nearby field, her senses were always on the alert for those small, subdued signs he might fail to detect and which could spell the difference between life and death.

Her speech was a product of the frontier, a blending of Scotch and Irish richly mixed with Teutonic expressions drawn from Prussian and Low German. But the underlying fabric of the backwoods language was Elizabethan English—the pithy, archaic tongue of the English masses, much of which still sounds in Central Appalachia.

In her twenty-ninth year Jenny Sellards Wiley had never seen a schoolhouse. She was a woman of the frontier, aware of its dangers, unafraid of its hardships. More than most frontier women she was at home in that vast sea of trees that challenged the brave and cunning and repelled or destroyed the weak and uncertain. And, like most whom she knew, some strange mystic influence moved within her so that her eyes looked often to the West, where the wild land stretched without limit.

CHAPTER TWO

Thomas Wiley had chosen well in selecting the land for his farm. In a decade of hard labor he had cleared forty acres. They lay at the mouth of a valley where the hills stood apart and the bottoms were black with ancient loam. In the beginning he had girdled the great trees and after the bark had begun to scale from their trunks they were brought down with fire and the axe.

The fields were enclosed with worm-rail fences. A barn had been raised, and pens for cattle, sheep, hogs and domestic fowls. Such enclosures were an absolute necessity on the frontier where wolves, bears and mountain lions were constantly on the prowl for prey.

The cabin stood near the base of the hill so all of the little farm could be seen from the front door. It was built of hewed poplar logs, joined with a precisely cut half-dovetail at the corners. There was one large room twenty feet wide and twenty-two feet long with a half-story in the loft. The loft was reached by ladder, pegged against a wall, which ascended through a hole in the ceiling.

To the rear of this structure stood a smaller cabin. The two buildings were joined together by a roofed and thick-walled "dog-trot." It was the only home of its kind in the settlement and to the other families shut up in a single, hopelessly crowded room, it represented sheer opulence.

Wiley did not have the passion for hunting that consumed virtually all other men in the settlement except Borders. He spent most of his time at work on his expanding fields, impelled by a vision of a broad farm yellow with wheat and corn and speckled with grazing herds. Such diligence had rewarded his family. Their farm, like their cabin, was the best on Walker's Creek.

He had hewed the logs of his house so skillfully that their edges joined, requiring little chinking. The floors were made of pegged yellow ash puncheons.

In one end of the larger cabin there yawned a cavernous fireplace with a huge stone lintel. The cooking was done on andirons and in cast-iron skillets and bakers on the glowing hearth. Above the fireplace hung one of the household's two rifles. The other lay on pegs over the door. Both were always loaded. There were two low beds in the loft and two slightly larger ones downstairs. In many frontier homes bedsteads were unknown luxuries, with Indian-style cornshuck pallets serving their function. But Wiley had laboriously carved out bedsteads for all members of the family and had fitted them with webs of taut ropes.

There were oaken, hickory-bottomed chairs and a walnut table with benches set along both sides. In a corner stood Jenny's loom, nearly always spread with cloth. And by the loom was her rocking cradle, now occupied by Adam, her youngest child, at fifteen months.

Jenny had three other children, George, her oldest, was ten, and had been named for the President. He was a nimble, sturdy boy with his father's features and attitudes.

Seven-year-old Elizabeth was her aunt's namesake. She was a serious, pretty dark-haired child remarkably like her mother in appearance.

And there was five-year-old Hezekiah, "called after his grandfather" and generally referred to simply as "Hez."

Jenny was pregnant again. The child within her had been growing for seven months. Many backwoods women had a child every year for two decades, and though Jenny had not maintained this record, before her thirtieth birthday she would have borne her fifth child.

There was one other member of the household, Jenny's fifteen-year-old half-brother, Andrew. He had acquired the frame of a man, broad-shouldered, black-haired, thick-chested. Already he had gone several times into the wilderness on "short hunts" of a week or ten days' duration, sometimes alone, sometimes with another boy or two. He had lived in the Wiley cabin a year, ever since his father went to live with his daughter, Elizabeth. His mother, the old man's second wife, was dead. Andrew's relationship to his sister was much like that of a son. Her fondness for him was immense and his willing strength contributed much to the security and growing prosperity of the household.

And the prosperity was discernible in the increasing herds of livestock. The Wileys now owned three horses and two good plow mules. They had two milk cows, a dozen sheep, at least twenty hogs and a hundred chickens, ducks and geese.

As important as any of these was the pack of dogs. There were six of them—vicious, ugly-tempered hounds and mastiffs. They were sentinels against marauding animals and even more bloodthirsty men.

There was another little fellow who generally remained

at Jenny's heels. He was half grown, a little black and white mongrel called Tige. Soon after he was born his mother was killed by a wolf and Jenny had had to feed him from a spoon. He repaid her kindness with an unswerving affection.

The Harmans and Skaggses had been planning for three years to leave the little settlement at the foot of Walker's Mountain and strike out down the long valley of the Tug Fork to the Big Sandy in the vast wilds of Kentucky. Their yearning for new lands was encouraged by the hoary Henry Harman, whose ancient heart still felt the tug of wanderlust. Tice Harman had been scouting the Big Sandy and its tributaries since he was eighteen. He first went there alone in 1755 on a long hunt that lasted nearly five months. For two hundred miles he had followed the winding Tug down to its union with the Louisa. Beyond, in the main valley of the Big Sandy River, he had found an abundance of game. In a ford he had seen so many buffalo wallowing in the shallow water that it was impossible for him to cross the stream and he had sat for hours watching the immense shaggy beasts. Thereafter Tice Harman and his brothers had scouted beyond the mountains all the way to the Mississippi, crossing that awesome flow of water on a raft to venture into plains as flat as a table top. They had wandered to the Cumberland and far southward into huge pine flats where the heat lay like an oppressive blanket. They had seen many astounding sights—huge herds of buffalo, clouds of wild birds, river catfish as long as a tall man—but the Harmans had turned their backs on them all to return to the Appalachians. The wild, empty and lush hills were the habitat they loved.

Then and on later forays to the Sandy Valley Tice Harman found many places well suited for settlement. Wide cane-covered valleys, immense trees, abundant mast of wild nuts, flocks of birds that sometimes blackened the sun, deer and elk by the thousands, black bears everywhere, sometimes a dozen or more hibernating in a single cave. Harman had always meant to go back to the Big Sandy (sometimes called the Great Sandy), to the Shawnees' "Valley of Mystery." Now after more than three decades, in his fifty-seventh year he was determined to brave all perils to move to a place near the Painted Licks, on the Louisa fork of the river. There he had found many salty streams bubbling out of the ground, and for five miles around them Indians had traced smooth-barked timber with red and black images of birds, animals and men. Harman detested the aborigines and believed steadfastly in their extermination. He coveted their valley and planned to plant a backwoods fort squarely in its center.

Jenny was generally content in the security of the home she and her husband had built. But sometimes when she heard Harman or Henry Skaggs describe the long Valley of Mystery and the immense Ohio flowing beyond its mouth she felt a strange disquiet, and the familiar fields and buildings suddenly appeared shrunken and insignificant.

Tom did not share this disquiet. His yearnings were for new fields adjoining those he had already cleared. Though he was sometimes enraptured by the enormous wilderness, the call to conquer it with bloodstained fingers did not sound in his heart.

The Irish brogue was on his tongue and the Irish sparkle was in his eyes. Good humor hovered about him and he showered jokes, riddles and jests on his family. When the people gathered for a house-raising or wedding or to celebrate a good crop year with drink and dancing. Tom

Wiley and his fiddle were at the center of the merriment. He toiled longer and harder than any of his backwoods neighbors but his spirit remained bright as his fields broadened.

He was the shoemaker for half the settlement, shaping ankle-high "Spanish pumps" for women and girls and boots and moccasins for men and boys. His hammer and awl were busy by the light of bear-grease candles until late at night. His nimble fingers shaped and colored toys of corn shucks, cobs and fine light wood. Soldiers, carts and whistles emerged in moments at the request of a child. And he could read a little and was a "fair scribe" with a pen, and these skills he sought to pass on to his and other children.

Sometimes, after a spirited Irish jig or reel, he turned his fiddle and his voice to a plaintive Old-World ballad— some story of love or war. Then he sang of "Greensleeves" or "King Henry's Lady." Again, with a dram of whiskey from the flask of a visitor, he would zestfully sing in a ribald vein of a lover's plea to his sweetheart, "Oh, Blow the Candle Out!"

Tom Wiley was happy where he was. Though Irish, he was not Catholic, but a pensive, sometimes devout quality showed through his character. Loving his valley, his farm and his family he was saddened by the growing talk of a new move to primordial western lands. He knew they would go and, sadly, he was resolved to remain behind and build the kind of farm an honest Irishman could be proud of. Sometimes as he worked he mused that his grandchildren might even have schools with books and a teacher. These were the frontiers toward which he moved.

CHAPTER THREE

As September waned, the men made plans for the autumn's major event—the "long hunt." They would spend a month or six weeks in the wilderness to the northwest of the settlement replenishing their larders and storing peltries for sale in the eastern trading posts.

Usually the hunt began in late October and continued until early in December, but this year there would be a prelude to it. The venerable Henry Harman knew he could never again experience the joys of a long hunt. Despite his great age his body was still remarkably strong, but the rigors of the trail and a six-week encampment in the wilderness were too much for him. Still, he yearned to feel the recoil of his massive rifle and to shake with the emotion that flowed into him when his hands shoved a keen blade into the jugular of a bear or buffalo. This year he urged his sons and neighbors to take him on a short hunt to a "bower" or hunting lodge they had built nearly twenty years before some forty miles away on the headwaters of the Tug. It was set in the formidable hills on the upper reaches of the Big Sandy where game was abundant, though less so than in the lower stretches of that vast primordial valley where the wide bottoms supported herds of buffalo and elk. There the patriarch could remain in the lean-to, or near it, and hunt from the open fields surrounding it and in the nearby forests, while the others went farther afield.

To "humor the old man," his sons and the Skaggses undertook a two-week foray. Upon their return they would remain a few days at the settlement and then go back to the valley. This time they would descend to its forks, make camp under one of the immense cliffs or "rockhouses" that line the riverbanks and hunt for a month longer. So in the last week of September eight of the men loaded pack horses with salt, gunpowder, cooking utensils, extra rifles, meal and parched corn and set forth into the wilderness. Henry Harman rode a surefooted mule.

At the end of the second day they came to the old camp. The lean-to was made of round logs notched together at the ends with the roof poles sloping toward the rear. It was roofed with huge slabs of oak and chestnut bark, which the men soon renewed. Eight or ten hunters could sleep in it, comfortably sheltered from the rain and wind. The front of the hut opened against an immense beech, effectively providing two entrances, one on either side of the trunk. The skins of bear and buffalo were spread on a thick layer of leaves.

At night a low fire burned nearby for heat and light, and at least one man stood sentinel with a mastiff bitch at his side.

The shelter was surrounded by a natural clearing, embracing about three acres. The land in front of it sloped down to the edge of the stream, which even in this upland teemed with fish. To the rear the clearing extended upward about two hundred yards to the base of the hill where a tangled thicket of rhododendron covered a dozen acres.

Four days before the hunters left Ab's Valley a band of Indians set out from Old Chillicothe for the Cherokee village far to the south in the highlands of the huge territory known as Tennessee. It was a strange mixed band drawn from four tribes. There were fourteen of them altogether—six Shawnees, two Wyandots, two Delawares and four Cherokees. The Cherokees had come visiting late in the summer, seeking recruits for raids against white settlements on the southern border.

The Shawnees were led by a grizzled old warrior and medicine man called Black Wolf. He had warred on the "white-eyes" for nearly forty years. He was at least sixty, the oldest man in the party.

The Wyandots and the Delawares had drifted westward during and after the Revolution when fierce fighting blazed along the frontier, and, with other segments of uprooted Indian nations, had attached themselves to the depleted Shawnees beyond the Ohio.

The Cherokees were a subchief named Dull Knife, and his teenage son, Little Black Bear, and two young braves. Dull Knife was a henchman of Chief Benge, the bloodthirsty half-breed whose name had terrorized a whole generation of backwoods settlers.

The Indians had known little but the hunting path and war trail since infancy. They were dressed in the curious garb then common to the tribes dependent on trade goods— buckskin leggings, shirts, and moccasins intermingled with garments of cheap red and blue cloth from the stores of French fur traders. Leather packs on their shoulders contained buffalo-skin robes for protection against the impending winter, salt, parched corn, and various items picked up by barter and plunder.

Dull Knife was a striking figure, much larger than his fellows, about fifty years of age. His coarse black hair bound into braids with small silver clasps, a necklace of flat silver disks hung from his neck, and a broad silver bracelet encircled each of his wrists. Bits of the metal were worked as ornaments into his leather jacket.

This show of vanity did not lessen the cruelty of his face or the smoldering hardness of his eyes. His lips were thick and full, his nose was somewhat flattened, and his eyes were set far apart. His short neck, broad square hand and sturdy legs betokened great strength and endurance. Dull Knife was a pathological killer in whom there burned tirelessly a hatred for all people with white skins. As a boy he had attached himself to a band of raiders who had struck from their fastness in the cloud-swept Carolina highlands deep into the Shenandoah Valley. When they returned with captives, he had won approval from the warriors for his inventiveness in devising new tortures for them. He had brought howls of glee from the Indians when he crept up behind a naked man bound for burning at the stake shoved a red-hot iron into his testicles.

On this journey his steps were dogged by his admiring son, a boy of seventeen. Tall, erect and handsome Little Black Bear was eager to take his first scalp. He was armed with a keen new steel hatchet and butcher knife, a bow of black locust and a score of iron-shod arrows.

There lay across Dull Knife's shoulder a silver-ornamented rifle, a trophy captured from a Virginia militia officer. His huge powder horn was similarly decorated. A pouch of bullets hung near his waist. During the Revolution he had for a time drawn the pay of a British sergeant—and, in the process, had acquired the sobriquet of "Captain John" by which he was known to many Indian fighters.

One of the Delawares carried a Brown Bess musket and a steel ramrod. With the exception of the Shawnee chief, the others were armed with the long, ungainly small-bore rifles turned out by Pennsylvania gunsmiths and sold across the western wilderness by traders. The usual price of such a weapon was a stack of fur pelts as high as the rifle was long. They were ominous-looking but were far less effective than the shorter, larger-bore firearms generally found in backwoods cabins.

Old Black Wolf was of slender build with fine, thin features and the calm impassive countenance of a Greek Stoic. No flicker of emotion crept across his graven features. His long straight nose, tight lips, high cheeks and copper skin were framed by graying locks that fell to his shoulders. He wore none of the ornamentation affected by the Cherokee. At his waist and from his shoulders hung a number of small bags, in which he collected roots, leaves, bits of mineral and other ingredients to be brewed for use in religious ceremonies and as medicinal herbals. He carried an excellent .40-caliber rifle, a gift from the British Crown which he had served tenaciously and with much guile through nearly a decade of warfare.

Black Wolf remembered, with a deep anguish which he bore in silence, the days of tribal greatness when the Shawnee nation had hunted upon and claimed sovereignty over an immense territory, and had acknowledged only the terrible Iroquois as their equals on the battlefield. But two generations of incessant warfare with other tribes and with land-hungry whites had reduced the tribe to a few villages north of the Ohio and scattered bands in the southern

Appalachians. Black Wolf knew within his soul that his people were doomed to fight and flee until the last was gone or survived only by sufferance of white overlords. Black Wolf would fight the inevitable so long as blood flowed in his icy veins. Like an old bear brought to bay by hunters he would die without any thought of surrender or self-pity.

The ten younger men were eager for adventure. Some had already plucked their hair into scalp locks and daubed their faces with black, red, blue, and yellow war paint. After a visit in the Cherokee village they would raid the white settlements and, if lucky, burn a blockhouse. Perhaps they could carry away some white women for squaws or to be sold to Canadian farmers for ransom. There were many sorts of desirable plunder to be picked up on the war trail—guns, axes, hatchets, mirrors, kettles, cloth, and whiskey.

As the late summer days of September ran out like beads dropping from a broken string, the band crept toward their goal, but soon a mischance would divert them onto other wilderness trails. They would not see the proud Cherokee council houses this year. Some would not see them at all.

On the second morning after the white hunters had made their camp at the old bower, they breakfasted on broiled meat and cornbread and all of them, except Henry Harman, left the camp. The Skaggs brothers and Robert Hawes went downstream to an area where much beech mast was falling and where deer were likely to graze. The Harmans and George Draper moved toward the east, planning to cross the headwaters of a small stream into an upland area where they expected to find bears, fat and ready for the winter hibernation. Quiet as a shadow the mastiff preceded them by a dozen yards. It was a little after daybreak when the last sound of their departure died in the ears of the grizzled Prussian.

But their leaving had not gone unobserved. The red men had spent the night under an overhanging cliff two miles downstream. Before daylight they were on the trail again, moving in a single file up the valley to the south. A Wyandot scout walking half a mile ahead had detected the cooking fire. He sped down the path to warn the others, who closed up and crept stealthily forward. By an all but invisible trail they found their way into the rhododendron thicket to the rear of the camp, and as the hunters departed, fourteen pairs of keen eyes observed their every movement.

They watched intently as the old man took up his position under the huge beech. He leaned his back against the trunk and waited, a loaded rifle across his knees. The sounds of the awakening forest surrounded him—the chirp and flutter of birds and the chatter of squirrels. From down the valley there came the low bellow of a buffalo, and a moment later from a distant ridgetop, the scream of a panther. The cry told the Indians that the great male mountain lion had found no prey during the night, and now, at daybreak, was both hungry and angry.

To Harman these sounds were like the soothing beat of sweet music. His arthritic joints threatened to immobilize his body, but his eyes and ears still measured the forest and a quick wit translated his perceptions into an almost instantaneous comprehension of its every movement. On occasion his hands could still be as steady as granite.

In the thicket, Dull Knife beckoned his son to him. Little Black Bear crouched by his father's side as the chief whispered that this was an opportunity for him to tie his first scalp to his belt. The others would remain in the thicket while the boy crept forward and took the scalp of the single hunter whose form could be seen by the tree. Dull Knife knew that he was old and correctly surmised that he was Tice Harman's father. The patriarch, too, carried a formidable reputation in the Cherokee nation, and was detested almost as much as his son. Harman the elder had long advocated the eradication of all Indians, a policy he had forthrightly advanced in militia councils, sometimes within earshot of Indian allies. Any warrior would be proud to display the old Indian-killer's scalp in the lodges of his people.

As Dull Knife prompted the youth, his ears told him that the last white man except old Harman was out of hearing. Within a few more moments he would be beyond the sound of a gunshot as well. Little Black Bear would creep forward, sink his tomahawk into the old man's skull and take the scalp as quietly as a breath.

Little Black Bear loosened his tomahawk in his belt and his butcher knife in its scabbard. Holding the stout bow with an arrow notched on the string, he stepped out along the dim trail leading from the thicket down to the edge of the stream. His father's eyes gleamed with pride and excitement as they followed his movements.

A quarter of a century before, during Chief Pontiac's great rebellion, his father and brother, both honorable men and great warriors, had fought by the side of Virginia militiamen. They had helped rout the Shawnee, Mingo, Delaware, Wyandot and Chippewa, accompanying their white allies all the way to the Forks of the Ohio. They had helped the militiamen burn French treading posts in order to deny arms to the Shawnee. In all things, they had remained faithful to the cause in which they had taken up arms. When the campaigns of that war ended, white and redmen returned along the same trails. His father and brother spent the night with their white comrades in arms in the shadows of the western mountains. After a celebration feast, they fell asleep around the same fire.

The forty Indians did not know when they wrapped themselves in their blankets that their white comrades had learned that in their absence the colonial government had published a bounty offer of ten pounds for the scalp of each hostile Indian taken during the war. The hostiles were, of course, the Shawnee and Delaware, but the scalp of a friendly Indian was indistinguishable from that of a foe. The unprincipled and half-savage borderers who composed the militia company counted four hundred pounds' worth of skin and hair on the heads of their Indian allies.

Turkey Feather, Dull Knife's distinguished father, his brother Wounded Buffalo and seven other Cherokees were tomahawked in their sleep. A yell awakened the others and they fled weaponless and half-naked to carry the tale of perfidy to the outraged tribe. The infuriated survivors insisted that Henry Harman and his sons were among the murderers.

Dull Knife had sworn in his heart that, so long as blood flowed through his flesh, there would be no peace between him and the white men. Necessity had forced him to continue to do business with the traders who circulated in the backwoods. He needed their weapons and their goods. But to those white men and women who spoke the English language, hungered for Indian lands, and built their wretched cabins ever deeper into the Appalachians and the grassy meadows beyond, he bore a bitter hatred. He had warred against them for a whole generation. Now his eyes gleamed with anticipation as his son set forth to even scores with the slayer of his grandfather.

He watched intently as the youth moved. No leaf or stick or blade of grass rustled beneath his moccasins. Dull Knife noted his progress with satisfaction. Not even a hunting owl could have moved more quietly, but his coming was not undetected. A flock of pigeons had settled to the ground in the clearing, picking at seeds scattered from wild grasses. As the youth approached, they took flight and flew past Harman. Their passage signaled to him that some large animal or man was in the vicinity. He twisted around and in an instant recognized his peril. The Indian boy was not alone; others would be watching from the woods. The direction of approach told him the others were in the thickets. He struggled to rise but his decrepit knees did not respond, He scrambled wildly and clumsily about, at last putting the butt of his rifle against the earth and pulling himself slowly upward by the barrel. While he was doing so, Little Black Bear lifted his short, heavy bow, drew back the string to his ear and released it with a low, ominous hum. There was a thudding sound clearly audible to the watchers in the thicket as the arrow plowed into the old man's chest. It penetrated about four inches and Harman grunted under the impact. The pain shot through him like a shaft of fire.

The boy uttered no sound. He flung the bow aside and jerked the hatchet from his belt. With one hand outstretched before him he leaped across the intervening space. But in that instant the resolve and some of the ancient strength that had always characterized the old Prussian returned to him. The cocked rifle came to his shoulder. For a fraction of a second it wavered uncertainly, then the gnarled hands tightened upon it. His eye, still glittering after eighty-six summers, sighted along the straight octagonal barrel. For a fleeting instant the silver foresight was aligned precisely with the V-shaped rear sight. The finger tightened on the trigger. There was a clack as the flint hit the frizzen, a flash and a roar, and Little Black Bear spun around and fell heavily on his face, a neat round hole in the center of his forehead.

The moccasined foot of the dying boy dug a little trench in the black loam, but before it stopped twitching the astounded and anguish-stricken Dull Knife was galvanized into action. Casting discretion aside, he shrieked a bloodcurdling war whoop and, issuing instructions to the braves, leaped down the trail toward his fallen son.

Others bounded after him, spreading out and advancing on a broad front. As they ran, their shouts and wails resounded through the forest.

But old Harman was neither dead nor in a mood to surrender. Agony ran through him in paralyzing waves but his wound was not mortal, and now that he was aroused, much of the purpose and energy of his long-departed youth surged back into him. Like an ancient chipmunk, he scurried into the bower where the four extra rifles lay loaded and primed. Seizing one of them, he returned in an instant to the entrance. A Delaware was bearing down upon him with a scalping knife in one hand and a rifle in the other. Again Harman's aim was unerring and the warrior went tumbling across the wild sward a dozen yards before coming to a halt on his back.

Breathing heavily, the patriarch grabbed another firearm and drew a bead on an Indian swooping in on him from the other side of the bower. When his rifle cracked this time, a chastised brave dashed back toward the thicket, his left arm flapping wildly.

Harman dragged his two remaining rifles to the back of the shelter, out of sight. The Indians, for their part, dashed for the nearby trees. This put them between the wounded Harman and the hunters. Only Dull Knife was behind the bower and Harman punched a hole through the roof in order to see in that direction. What he beheld was the brawny chief disappearing into the thicket with the lifeless body of his son.

The Cherokee carried his burden along the gloomy arched passage that laced through the rhododendron and came out on the hillside above. There a huge beech had turned up in a storm, creating a deep mossy sinkhole. He placed the body in it and gazed for a moment at the still features. The eyes were closed, the lips open in a faint smile. He wiped away the blood clotting on the forehead and in the eyebrows. Suddenly his heart, tempered to bloodshed, torture, and hatred in a lifetime of warfare, broke with frustration and grief. A deep convulsive sob shook him as he rubbed the boy's hair against his face.

Then he sprang up and resumed the fray. Now he knew for certain the identity of the man in the shelter and of most of the others hunting beyond in the forest. They were the Indian-hating Harmans and their land-hungry neighbors—the same vile and cunning crew who had thwarted him so often in the past. His overpowering impulse was for vengeance against the killer of his offspring and against all people of their blood and race.

In the meantime the resourceful Harman had managed to break off the cedar arrow shaft just above the spike head, and this afforded him increased freedom of movement. Lying inside the shelter, he was invisible to the encircling Indians. He knew that unless help returned very soon they would rush him, and that his throat would be cut and his scalp torn from his skull within a moment of their arrival. With one cocked rifle in his hand and the other across his knees he was determined to take at least one more "varmint" with him into the next world.

But Harman, who had eluded the grim reaper so many times before, would escape his scythe again. The hunters had heard the shots and were returning. The Skaggs party had gone only a few hundred yards when they caught sight of a herd of deer leisurely feeding toward them up the stream. They waited in the undergrowth for the animals to come within rifle range. They were there when they heard the shots and war whoops and immediately ran back toward the camp.

The four Harmans and George Draper were only a little farther away when they passed an immense hollow poplar. Claw marks and tufts of hair on its inner surface indicated that a huge bear, fat for winter hibernation, had climbed up the column to find shelter. They were standing about the tree discussing possible methods of bringing him down without the labor of felling the tree when the sounds of the battle reached them.

Within minutes the two bands were locked in furious combat. A half-dozen bullets had plowed harmlessly into the log walls of the shelter when the Indians suddenly diverted their fire to the new targets.

George Harman's rifle misfired as a Shawnee bore down upon him with a long, glittering knife in his hand. They grappled and fell heavily to the ground. Harman gripped the warrior by the wrist of his knife hand and managed to stay the blade a few inches from his throat. With a titanic effort he got the head of the warrior under his arm and gripped it in a viselike hold. In the position they tumbled about, grunting with hate and fury.

Presently the Indian sank his teeth into a fold of flesh on Harman's side. In a final paroxysm of fury and outrage Harman drove the red man's tightly clenched fist downward, inflicting a bloody wound in the warrior's leg. The Indian dropped the knife, tore loose from his adversary's grip and began chipping at the white man's head and neck with a tomahawk. A glancing blow severed an ear and peeled a broad fold of flesh from the side of Harman's head. Misjudging the severity of the wound, the Shawnee closed for the kill and the blood-and-sweat-soaked borderer plunged a knife into the base of his neck.

A bullet struck Robert Hawes in the elbow, shattering his arm. Unable to reload his rifle and helpless to defend himself from an encounter with knife or hatchet, he fled into the forest and hid in a small patch of wild cane. George Draper brought down upon his name a shame that has stained it to this day. He fled up a little spur to the trail leading southward toward the settlement. Half a mile away he hid in a cave and did not rejoin the others until late in the afternoon, long after the Indians had left the field.

The Indian leaders had seen too many of their people perish in struggles of this kind to keep up the contest for long. Their tribes were too depleted to afford the sacrifice of men. Once they had counted warriors in the thousands. Now their war parties rarely numbered more than a few dozen. Despite his grief and towering rage, Dull Knife was compelled to join the more cautious Black Wolf in signaling the braves to withdraw. Like dying whispers, they suddenly vanished into the forest, leaving two of their number sprawled in death at the bower.

None of the white men had been killed, but three were seriously injured and one had ignominiously "skedaddled."

In addition, two of their tethered horses had been shot and the others had been driven off into the wilderness. Henry Harman's patient mule had disappeared with a loud hee-haw. The hunters were reluctant to venture into the woods in search of the animals. It was a thoroughly shaken party that gathered by the edge of the little clearing.

The first consideration was to care for the wounded. Hawes's arm was placed in a rude splint. His pain was intense, but they could afford him no relief except for a couple of deep draughts from a whiskey flask.

The ancient Harman was a much more urgent problem. Incredibly, the arrow had missed both lungs and heart, and now it had to be withdrawn. Tice drew it out as deftly as possible and the old man endured with a deep gasp pain that would have made most young men swoon. Heavy bleeding began and an attempt was made to stanch it by packing the opening with cold bear lard and a compress made of a torn shirt.

For George Harman nothing more could be done than to tie the fold of skin back into its proper place, rub his many cuts and bruises with bear grease and set him on his feet.

Both Tice Harman and his father had recognized their old adversary, Captain John. They had known and detested him for many years and surmised with considerable satisfaction that the young man slain by the first shot was his son. They could imagine the full flood of his fury and the lust for vengeance that would now impel him to Walker's Creek. And the form his retribution would take against white people falling into his clutches could be visualized in all its searing agony. Not a moment could be lost in returning the battered band to the settlement and to its defense.

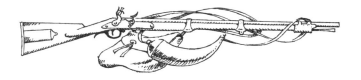

CHAPTER FOUR

October 1 dawned crisp and clear with a threat of frost in the air. Tom Wiley rose before daylight and loaded a pack horse for a trip across the ridges to the east to a trading post twenty miles away. During the spring and summer, he and his family had dug roots of ginseng from the mountain coves. These herbs were valued in the Orient for their medicinal properties, and he would exchange them for salt, coffee, lead, and powder. The trip would require a long day and he would not get back to his cabin until long after nightfall.

Jenny cooked breakfast for him, spreading the table with cornbread, butter, honey, fried pork, and eggs. With a packet of the same rough fare in his pocket for his dinner at noon, he mounted another horse. Jenny handed up his rifle and powder horn and he rode away in the first faint rays of the new day. Before going he leaned down from the saddle to kiss his wife goodbye and she clung to him for a moment in an embrace that would always haunt his memory.

With the ascending sun, the day warmed and the air filled with the droning sounds of autumn. Insects hummed and murmured and leaves fluttered slowly to the earth. Tom was rarely absent and Jenny missed him. A vague foreboding hung over the cove—an eerie air characteristic of late summer, that hazy season before the first frosts, when the Indians so often struck the warpaths.

Andrew and George spent the morning at household chores. They milked the cows and brought in the last of the potatoes from the field and stored them in the loft. They cut the stalks of corn in the vegetable garden and bound them for fodder. Jenny sat at her loom weaving threads of yellow, blue, and red into a piece of sturdy cloth. When the cloth was finished, she would sew it into a dress for her daughter.

Soon after midday a black thunderhead appeared in the western sky. Thunder rolled and lightning flashed in an unseasonal storm. But the storm did not strike. Instead the temperature dropped and a slow, steady drizzle commenced. Dampness and a chill crept into the house and she directed that fresh wood be piled on the fire. The children settled themselves on shuck mats before the hearth, to while away the hours with games. Andrew began carving a whistle for his nephew.

The dogs huddled under a shed near the chimney. About the middle of the afternoon, they began baying and growling and Jenny surmised that some large animal was passing on the ridge to the south. With deep-throated snarls and barks, they pursued the creature and their savage chorus died out as they passed through a distant gap. Only little Tige remained and he crept in and curled up by the hearth.

The leaden afternoon wore on. About four o'clock a knock rattled the door, and when Jenny lifted the latch bar John Borders stood before her. He was drenched and sat for a half hour before the fire. One of his sheep was missing and he had crossed the hill looking for it. He smoked a pipeful, listening to the drumming of the rain and the hissing as drops came down the chimney. He was obviously disturbed and, as he knocked out his pipe, explained why. While he was on the ridge separating their cabins, he had heard the hooting of owls. The calls came from at least four different places and sounded authentic enough. He had stood a long time under a cliff listening to them, and while he could not define the cause of his suspicion, the conviction grew upon him that the sounds were not genuine. The hour was a bit too early, he thought, and there were too many of the creatures. "Jenny," he said with finality, "I think there are Indians about."

He urged her to get the children ready and cross the ridge with him to his cabin. The distance was only a mile and he would be much more at ease with Tom Wiley's household under his roof. Besides, in returning Tom would have to pass the Border's cove and they could listen for his horse's hooves and bring him, too, to the cabin for the night.

Jenny discounted his fears. She, too, had heard the dismal cries and they had disturbed her. She was concerned, too, by the fact that the vicious and watchful dogs were away from the cabin and could not be relied upon to warn of an attack. Still, Jenny was stout-hearted. On the frontier one could not flee at every ominous portent, because danger could be construed hourly from some forest sound. Steady nerves were required of a backwoods wife. Her rifle hung dry and ready above the fireplace and a honed axe lay by the bed. Her cloth was needed but unfinished and she wanted to complete her task. She urged Borders to remain before the fire until he was warm and dry and promised that she would be watchful and would come to his home later if anything happened to alarm her further. A few moments later Borders picked up his long rifle and left, urging her to reconsider and follow him before darkness fell.

As the afternoon wore on to darkness Jenny plied her loom with an indifferent hand. The cabin was dry and warm. The rain beat forlornly upon the roof and walls. The older children lay contentedly before the fire while her brother entertained them with improvised toys and with stories, tricks and riddles. Wrapped in a panther-skin blanket the baby, Adam, slept peacefully in his cradle. Jenny alone was not at peace. Steadily the conviction grew on her that all was not well. Suddenly, at dusk, she resolved to go to the Borders cabin. She opened the door and looked at the darkening hills. The deep, raucous hooting of an owl came from the nearby timber. She whistled for the missing dogs, but there was no response. Tige ran out the door past her, standing in the rain for a moment with his ears cocked toward the forest. He barked furiously, then ran back into the house.

Reentering, she dropped the bar across the door behind her. Curtly she told Andrew to help her get the children ready to cross the ridge. He and they murmured protests but promptly gathered before the fire pulling on jackets, shawls and caps.

With a heart-stopping crash the door flew inward, shattering the oak beam that lay across it. A heavy timber Tom Wiley had brought to the rear of the house for firewood shot through the thick portal. The iron hinges tore loose from the wood and the door fell with a splintering rattle onto the puncheon floor. A tide of human forms surged into the room and fell upon the little band gathered by the hearth. High-pitched, palpitating war cries filled Jenny's ears, followed by the quick crunch of a descending hatchet as it crushed through her half-brother's skull. A little geyser of blood and brains erupted from the falling body and fell hissing into the fire. In his agony he voiced a single sputtering cry. In a second or two, a bronzed arm flashed a long knife in his skull; a strong hand seized the black hair in a tight grip. The biceps in a muscular arm rolled upward and with a ripping sound the scalp parted from the battered skull. Shoved heavily backward, the dying boy writhed and kicked across the puncheons, abandoned by the sturdy savage who, with the bloody scalp in his hand, advanced upon the horrified Jenny. With a scream she sprang forward to interpose herself between the men and her children, but she was rudely checked by the heavy hands that seized her wrists and forearms, pinioning them behind her back in grips of iron. Hatchets and knives rose and fell. Above a babel of yells and hoots sounded a single piercing cry of "Mother! Mother!" The terrified eyes of her daughter caught her own, then a shaggy, wet buffalo hide on the shoulders of a warrior sprang between them and when the Indian turned a few seconds later to face Jenny he held the child's dripping scalp in his blood-soaked fingers.

Within thirty seconds of their entry across her threshold the savages had butchered the last of her children except the baby. He was discovered by the burly warrior who had tomahawked her brother. He seized the infant by his heels with the apparent intention of dashing his brains out against the wall.

When the baby was discovered and brought forward for execution a stern guttural voice rang out near her loom. There stood an older man of vast and commanding dignity. Tall, slender, authoritative, his hair parted in the middle and drawn severely down on either side of his head, wrapped in an immense buffalo robe that dripped water on the floor, his raised hand stayed the savage who held her baby. He continued to grip the infant by the heels while a spirited conversation ensued.

Benumbed with horror, shock and dread, her breath coming in deep, gasping drafts between parted lips, she listened to the debate between the two savages. She had considerable knowledge of the Cherokee tongue. The border was alive with halfbreeds who divided their time between white and red society. Big Jim, a Cherokee, had stayed many nights at the home of her father in her girl-hood and had stopped more than once at the Wiley cabin. He always brought fresh meat from the forest and was not unwelcome in most households. His mother was a squaw and his father a Scotch fur trader. From him and others she had learned much of the language. She comprehended at once that the killer of her brother was a Cherokee. The other, the older man now argued that her child should be spared, she took to be a Shawnee.

The Cherokee turned on Jenny a look of withering malevolence and hatred. He, like the Shawnee whom he addressed, was much older than the other warriors who thronged the room. Silver disks and bands bedecked his wrists, forehead, hair and clothing. Blood spattered his leather jacket and the cotton trade shirt beneath it. In his left hand, the wailing infant hung head downward, twisting and squirming in pain and outrage. His lip curling with scorn, he slapped the woman across the face with the gruesome trophy in his right hand and blood ran down her cheeks and the salty taste of it clung to her lips. "White bitch," he raged at her in English, "you Harman's wife?"

CHAPTER FIVE

For an interval that dragged on like a glacial age the two chiefs discussed her fate. At the beginning she had difficulty grasping the intent of their conversation, but her small knowledge of the Cherokee tongue and the gestures and facial expressions of the two savages quickly disclosed the substance of their grim debate.

The Cherokee wanted to kill the child and his mother without delay. He invoked the spirits of his son, newly dead, and of his murdered father and brother, and he reiterated the hatred of all Indians for Harman. With impassioned eloquence he denounced the white man's continuing encroachments onto tribal hunting lands.

The Shawnee urged a more lenient course. He pointed out that the Cherokee's vengeance was already considerable. One young man and three children were dead and a child and a sturdy squaw were captives. The woman would be valuable indeed in the Shawnee towns beyond the Ohio. And it could do no harm to spare her child, for he might prove to be a stout-hearted lad. In such event he could be adopted into the tribe, his poisonous paleface blood purified by ceremonies and incantations. The tribe was much depleted in numbers and it was wise to pick up new recruits when and where possible. But there was another matter that weighed heavily with him. The old warrior pointed to the loom. He was fascinated by the bright cloth and asserted that he wanted to take the white woman to his town and have her teach his squaws to weave in the same manner. A loom could be acquired by trade or capture and all the women of the tribe could learn this useful skill. With game diminishing, weaving and flax cultivation could be a boon. If she lagged on the trail, it would be an easy matter to slay her then.

During all this colloquy, Jenny stared into the faces of the disputants and the other warriors. With an obscene impudence they filled her house, straddling the forms of her murdered children and holding her in an unflinching grip that precluded resistance or struggle. Several of the younger men had plucked their scalp locks, leaving only a knot of hair into which was bound white, gray, and black eagle feathers. These warriors had painted their faces with the hideous war masks of their tribes. They leered and grimaced at her through grotesque colorations. Slate-blue, black, yellow, red, and white paint had been laid on in fantastic circles and slashes. The rain had moistened it and the paint had commenced to run, making the faces even more repulsive. Occasionally one of the braves punched her viciously with his fingers or the handle of a tomahawk. Outrage, grief and fury tore through her like floods of lava, threatening to burst her temples and extinguish her consciousness. But strangely, intervals of calm came occasionally, in which she noted with detachment the dusty dryness of her throat and the massive hammering of her pulse.

The outraged baby continued to shriek and writhe, and to silence it the silver-bedecked Cherokee suddenly pitched him into his mother's arms. His cries subsided and with occasional deep hiccups he gazed with round, inquisitive eyes at the grim figures.

The argument took a new turn. The old Shawnee insisted that the band should leave the area and head back to the Ohio. He pointed repeatedly to the north. Indians should never attack, he said, when surprise was wanting. Harman was on his way back to the settlement and might arrive at any moment. The old man had probably died and the mounted band would travel rapidly. Consequently, it would not surprising if Harman and his band of avengers were to overtake them within an hour or two. In such event, there would be a hard fight with the probability of sharp losses to the Indians. True, they would kill some white men, but that was not enough. Most of the Indians were young and reckless. Harman and his settlers were mature and experienced fighters. To risk an open clash would invite disaster.

He urged that they wait until the alarm certain to arise from the battle and the raid had subsided. The white men will go out in force and heavily armed, he declared, and failing to find the woman and her abductors, will become disheartened and return. In the meantime new recruits could be sought by the raiders and within two moons a massive new attack could be made, aimed this time at several cabins at once and wreaking a terrible vengeance. She heard the name "Benge" repeated several times and surmised that the aid of his band of marauders would be sought.

In a phrase sometimes used by her father, it became apparent that the "list of the wind" was with the wrinkled

Shawnee. Despite their ferocious actions and appearance most of the savages appeared anxious to avoid another encounter with Harman in the near future. Occasionally one of them would add his voice to the argument and eventually all but three indicated that they agreed with Black Wolf.

With a grunted acquiescence to the demands of his fellows, the Cherokee turned again to the woman. Seizing her long braids, he jerked her head far back and looked with black sadistic eyes deep into her own. Through gritted teeth and drawn lips he demanded a second time, "White slut, you Harman's wife?"

"No, no," she screamed, "this is not Tice Harman's house. I am the wife of Tom Wiley. You have killed his children!"

"Where Tom Wiley?" he demanded, shaking her until her teeth rattled like clicking dice.

"He has gone back to the trading post. He is not with Harman," she gasped. The room spun dizzily and a sickening, fiery knot of misery struck into her stomach like an uncoiling spring. She bit her lip and strove to retain consciousness. To swoon now was to suffer the scalping knife and seal the fate of her only remaining child. Under a supreme exercise of will, her nerves began to unwind a bit and the bizarre sights and sounds assumed all the horror of reality.

Her reply mollified her tormentor somewhat and with a final shove he released her. After a last babel of discussion, the raiders began plundering the cabin.

Braves seized pillows from the beds, slit them open and dumped the feathers onto the floor, thus converting the ticks into sacks. They prowled through the house looking into every nook and cranny for things of value. Scissors, thimbles, awls, cups, knives, forks and spoons were dumped into the bags. One warrior armed himself with the rifle above the fireplace. Dull Knife—for Jenny had detected the Cherokee's name—located a small box of silver coins her husband had kept on a shelf. With evident delight, he dumped them into a leather pouch that hung from his waistband. Two silver spoons brought from Ireland by her grandfather Sellards found their way into the same bag.

A warrior seized Tom Wiley's fiddle from its peg on the wall and began sawing the bow across the strings, while others laughed and clapped their hands with glee at the impromptu minstrel. After the laughter subsided he dropped the instrument into the leather pack he carried on his back. Meanwhile the Old Shawnee produced a long rawhide thong which he wrapped twice around Jenny's body just under the arms, and bound with a knot in front. Tables were broken and the splintered boards were heaped with chairs against the cabin wall and firebands were drawn from the hearth and stuck amid the tinder. Flames leaped up, casting a yellow light over the macabre scene—the dead, scalped, bleeding children, the grotesque faces of the warriors, the floor white with swirling feathers. The cabin caught fire and the savages filed through the splintered doorway. The last to go was Black Wolf, tugging on the rope to drag the distraught woman after him. In her arms she carried her child, sheltered, so far as she could manage it, by a woolen shawl. The rain-drenched night swallowed the curious procession, while behind them light from the burning cabin lit up the cove.

Dull Knife led the way to the north, ascending a long ridge that ran down to the valley behind the Wiley farm. The night was as dark as a cave and the rain continued to fall in leaden torrents. The braves followed one another in single file, and no word escaped them. The only sound was the muted padding of moccasined feet on the forest mold. Black Wolf brought up the rear, followed only by his tethered captive whom he jerked savagely when she slowed or stumbled.

The rain was cold and Jenny was dressed in woolen garments. In the manner of the day, she wore a great weight of clothing. She had on an outer garment that fell almost to the ground, gathered at the waist and spreading outward bell-fashion at her ankles. Under this was a petticoat of home-loomed linsey-woolsey, and next to her body were drawers of linen. None of the garments afforded any protection against the deluge. As they absorbed water, her clothes dragged at her with benumbing weight. The woolen shawl was little more than a trap for the rain and the soaked infant promptly commenced to kick and wail.

Within moments after they left the cabin, she was drenched to the skin. The water ran down her legs into her shoes. The icy flood chilled her to the bone and her teeth began clicking together uncontrollably. The Indians were protected by their buffalo robes but, notwithstanding, were quickly soaked almost as thoroughly as their prisoners. Still no word of complaint escaped any of them. Silently, stolidly, tirelessly, they plodded through the forest. When Jenny stumbled over a root or stone, Black Wolf pulled upon the rope and admonished her to hasten. And she knew from the outset that hasten she must, because the very moment when she and her child became a drag upon the escaping band, both would be tomahawked and scalped. Consequently, she made a superhuman effort to keep up. The child was a sturdy toddler weighing more than twenty pounds, and the task of carrying such a protesting burden would have taxed the strength of a muscular man. She neither expected nor received aid or sympathy. She shifted the child from one position to another and, as the march continued, her arms and shoulders turned to lumps of agony.

As the hours advanced, her pregnancy added immeasurably to her suffering. The baby in her womb kicked and squirmed as distressingly as the outraged infant in her arms. Her distended abdomen made it difficult to retain her balance on the rough terrain, so that she stumbled often and sometimes fell. A number of times she toppled forward, rolling upon the earth and allowing the child to slip from her grasp. On her hands and knees she crawled to the screeching infant while Black Wolf drew upon the rope and growled invectives and threats.

The Indians threaded their way through the darkness with remarkable ease, guided past precipices and fallen trees by subtle and highly developed senses. But the distraught and harried woman collided with trees and undergrowth and was tugged at by vines, branches and stones. Her feet, encased in heavy homemade shoes and saturated stockings, began to blister at the heels. Each step became excruciating, an exercise in sheer misery and will.

The trail led to the head of the tributary of Walker's Creek. After a few miles they left the ridge, crossed the intervening valley, and climbed the precipitous slope on the other side to the top of that ridge. They followed the rocky crest for two hours, then descended the steep and trailless mountain to the valley, and, for at least an hour, walked in the bed of a swift and swirling stream. Jenny knew they were making a determined effort to leave no trail and their shifting from ridge to ridge and their adherence to the swollen creek was calculated to eradicate or hopelessly confuse all signs of their passage. For that reason at every opportunity she dug her shoe heel into the earth or snapped off a trailing branch. Once in rising after a fall she stripped a small limb from a tree and managed to drop bits of it by her footsteps. But Black Wolf detected the stratagem and threatened to scalp her if she repeated it. The discovery of her ruse added little to her enormous woe. With Tice Harman and other really adept trackers and woodsmen away from the settlement, there were no highly skilled eyes to seek out her trail. The absent hunters were not expected to return for a fortnight. John Borders, Tom and the other men and boys at Walker's Creek would simply be unable to find her trace, especially after hours of heavy rainfall had washed each track. The direction of the flight could only be guessed at—whether toward the Shawnee north or the Cherokee south. Still, despite her rationalization, she ground her shoe heel into the earth whenever she could do so without attracting the attention of the sharp-eyed Black Wolf. She was puzzled by the references to a battle and to the Cherokee's dead son she had overheard in the debate between the two chiefs. Even if the savages had encountered Harman and the hunters near the latter's Big Sandy camp so that they were now headed back to the settlement, the fact could afford her scant hope. The wilderness was so vast and intricate that so skilled a hunter as Tice Harman or Henry Skaggs could search it in vain for the silent band that now led her relentlessly toward the north.

Vast as was her physical agony, her mental anguish exceeded it. The grief and shock induced by the frightful murders of her brother and three children were im-measurable, tearing at her spirit like red-hot irons laid on lacerated flesh. The spectacle of their twisted and bloody forms recurred endlessly before her eyes. Through her own shattering sense of loss welled a choking sympathy for her husband who, within hours, would come home to find all the members of his family dead or kidnapped and his home destroyed. But as a practical and resolute daughter of a hard and pragmatic people, Jenny knew that the all-important consideration now was not sorrow for those dead, but a determination to preserve her life and, with it, that of the infant sobbing in her arms. To accomplish this end, she had to be unflichingly brave, resilient, determined, and resourceful. To weaken, to indulge even for a moment in self-pity and the pitiless tomahawks would claim them within hours. The loss of her other children vastly magnified and constantly renewed her strength in the preservation of the one left to her.

But she had no illusions about her future. If she and the child lived, they would be carried to a village in Ohio, probably Old Chillicothe, where for years she would toil as a slave for the squaws. She would plant, till, and harvest corn, skin animals and tan hides for leather and laboriously sew them into jackets and leggings. She might be allowed to keep her child for a year or two, or the impulsive Indians might snatch him from her arms and hand him over to some squaw whose child had died. She could nurse the slender hope that eventually her captors would carry her off to Canada and sell her to a farmer or trapper. In the event of such good fortune, she would be bound to a legal servitude of five to seven years to repay the purchaser the ransom laid out in her behalf. The child would almost certainly grow up as a young Shawnee, as wild as his playmates and destined to die in warfare against the people of his own blood.

And, there was the ever-present possibility of torture.

If the Indians became provoked with her or drunk on captured whiskey, or if for any reason they fell into a bloodthirsty mood, they might kill her by an ordeal maddening to contemplate.

Another possibility, however, buoyed her up: slender and unlikely though it was, she might escape and return through the mountains to her husband and friends.

Even this frail glimmer of hope was appalling. The distances to be traveled would be huge. She would be unarmed in a wilderness filled with savage beasts and her track would be dogged by even more savage men who would relish the chase. She would have to ford wide rivers without boat or raft. If she lost her way in the labyrinth of hills and valleys she might wander for months or even years without encountering a white face. And if she failed—if she could not outwit and elude her pursuers—there would be the stake and fire. The likelihood of her coming again to the arms of her husband and to a new cabin was insignificant, but from the beginning of her ordeal it was her goal and she would never forsake it.

After about seven hours, the infant could weep no more and fell into an exhausted slumber. By that time, she was sustained by willpower alone. Her feet were swollen and her legs were without sensation. Despite the constant rainfall her lips were dry. She was feverish and felt a severe cold coming on. She trudged along, a wooden automaton too weary to fall and sometimes unable to remember where she was and why she persisted. As she felt the weariness of utter exhaustion coming over her, the Indians abruptly left the trail and turned up a narrow defile. A few moments later they stopped under a huge overhanging cliff. Dry firewood lay under the shelter, gathered by these or other marauders on earlier occasions. One of the Shawnees managed to start a fire which soon blazed up with much heat. Others managed to reduce the light by masking the flames with a screen of sticks and wet buffalo robes. Somehow she found the strength to remove her shoes and place her feet and stockings near the fire. Then, sodden and sick and indescribably weary, she collapsed into deep sleep.

CHAPTER SIX

From a slumber that was all too brief, Jenny was rudely awakened to find the form of Black Wolf, the Shawnee, bending over her. As she looked into his wrinkled face and cold penetrating eyes the nightmare of the previous night engulfed her again in a flood of horror and revulsion. She recoiled from the smell of their bodies—a mingling of sweat, grease, smoke and dirty leather. The dust of the rockhouse clung to their garments, turning them to an ashen gray.

The Indians were preparing for another long march. The fire had died to a low flame and the laurel thicket beyond the rockhouse was steeped in predawn darkness. The rain had stopped but water dripped from the edge of the cliff and the stream roared in torrential fury. The chill gripped the nape of her neck and her shoulders shook with a vast, involuntary heave.

As Jenny sat up she found that her outer garments, in close proximity to the fire, had dried but her undergarments were still clammy and wet. Mercifully, her feet, stockings and shoes were dry also. Her shoes had stiffened and as she pulled them onto her sore and swollen feet they pinched the blisters on her heels and toes. Her first thought was of escape—of flight with her child across the grim ridges to Walker's Creek. But the warriors stirred on light and nimble feet while her own creaked with stiffness and cold. A contest on such uneven terms could end only in certain disaster.

As she struggled to rise, she lost her balance and rolled ignominiously on the dusty ground, much to the delight of one of the warriors. He patted his own abdomen, then pointed to Jenny's protruding front. He grimaced and grunted and groaned like a squaw in labor. But his mirth vanished before the silence and disdain of his fellows.

The child awakened and began to squirm in a restlessness that Jenny knew signaled hunger, and after her long night of strenuous walking she, too, was faint from lack of food.

She felt a surge of gratitude and consolation when she discovered Tige near her side. He stood before her, his tail wagging and his eyes filled with questioning, a whining lump of devotion and expectancy. She stroked his head and back, apprehensive that the Indians would disapprove of his presence, but they ignored him, and when they left the camp the pup was permitted to accompany her. And he would stay not far from her heels, a faithful and affectionate friend, through countless vicissitudes and disasters which even now she could not foresee.

A Shawnee unbound his deerskin pack and began to distribute rations. He handed to each of the warriors long thin strips of blackened meat which Jenny recognized as jerky, or smoke-dried venison. Each piece was approximately an inch in width, an eighth of an inch thick, and about a foot long. Each warrior received two strips of it. Another Indian distributed parched corn, a cupped double handful per man.

Jenny received the same ration. Placing the corn in one of the pockets of her outer garment, she followed the example of the Indians and found a long slender stick. She wrapped the strips of meat around one end and held it in the flame until it was broiled. She then unwrapped the scorched and unappetizing mess from the stick and ate it with grains of the parched corn from her pocket. The meat had been smoked without salt, but salt had been added to the corn. It was rough fare, but Jenny's famished stomach welcomed it. Having nothing better to give the child, she pulled the jerky into small pieces and fed them to him, fearing all the while that he would choke on the hard and unfamiliar fare. But he gulped it down eagerly and begged for more. Black Wolf watched her intently and handed her another strip of the venison. She gave the wistful dog a little of the meat she had reserved for herself.

The Indians permitted her to leave the camp, to go as much as fifty yards away. There she washed her face in the cold stream and attended to her morning toilet. She was not spied on or molested on this or any similar occasion. She returned to the camp as promptly as possible and indicated that she was ready to resume the march. Her joints were stiff and sore and even before they left the camp her fatigue pressed upon her like a crushing weight. Her chest ached and blood pounded in her ears with each beat of her pulse. Her mouth felt puffy and a sore spot lay like a fiery ulcer at the base of her tongue. But as the savages shouldered their packs and rifles she resolutely picked up her offspring and squared her shoulders. The wife of Tom Wiley and the daughter of Hezekiah Sellards was not prepared to die easily.

The fire was extinguished and soiled and leaves were carried from the forest and dumped on the embers in an effort to make the camp appear much older than it was. Led again by the tireless Dull Knife, they plunged into the darkness.

When they left the camp the first gray glimmers of dawn were apparent on the eastern ridges. Slowly the fog lifted and the sunrise was chilly and cloudless. Again Black Wolf grasped the leather thong and pulled Jenny after him and again she carried the restless child and struggled to keep up.

They climbed the hill to its crest and followed it northward. Daylight found them on a high, sharp, rocky ridge. There Dull Knife and Black Wolf designated two warriors who disappeared to the southward. From their low tones and furtive expressions Jenny concluded that they had been dispatched as spies to keep a lookout for white pursuers. Suddenly, the stricken woman started with a flicker of new hope. Perhaps, despite the almost immeasurable odds against it, a pursuit had been mounted so swiftly and surely that the Indians had reason to feel uneasy. If so, hope and apprehension would henceforth grow together, because Indians habitually slaughtered their captives as soon as a rescue was attempted. Desperate as was her plight now, it would worsen immensely if the Dutchmen should work a miracle and track them down over a cold trail and through a gigantic labyrinth of hills and valleys.

Through the morning, they followed the crest of the ridge in a direction that was almost due north. Again Jenny felt the pangs of hunger and her child wept with fever and famine. It became apparent that adequate nourishment for the child would have to be found soon or it would die. His fever worsened and she felt a new surge of soreness rising in her throat and chest. Her eyes and nose began to run.

She was a pitiable spectacle when they stopped at noon for a brief rest and a little food.

This time only the ration of parched corn was distributed. Jenny ate her handful of the salted kernels slowly and carefully. They then left the path to find a small drain where the Indians dropped to their hands and knees and drank heavily. Jenny did likewise. Then, without a word, they resumed the trek.

The blisters burst on Jenny's heels and the liquid in them ran out into her stockings. Perspiration soaked her and her fever soared. She was in extreme distress and felt the last reserves of will and strength ebbing away. Her sole hope that the Indians would make an early camp and that one of them would provide ample food for the child and herself. Otherwise, the dawn would find her unable to move and this day would be her last.

In midafternoon Dull Knife led them down a long ridge to its terminus in a canebrake. A threadlike path wound through the cane, across a savage little stream and up the hillside beyond. As the warriors ascended the rough slope the path proved almost too much for the captive. Her heart thumped, her lungs ached, and she wheezed in an openmouthed struggle to maintain the pace. Her thoughts became incoherent and she fell into a trancelike stupor. More and more Black Wolf pulled the rope, each such gesture accompanied by a shake of his head and a muttered warning. He pointed toward Dull Knife and ran his finger across his throat. "White squaw, keep up!" he said repeatedly.

And Jenny strove mightily in obedience to his warning. Through the dreary, agonizing afternoon only an iron will sustained her. It kept her heart pounding and her rubbery legs churning while they climbed a long rocky ridge, followed it for more than four miles, then descended through a wooded cove to the headwaters of another stream. Here Dull Knife led the band into the creek bed and they walked in the clear, swirling water for another mile or two. At last, when she was so breathless and spent that the tomahawk no longer held terror for her, they came to the "mouth of the creek"—where it debouched into a much larger one. There, on their right, was a large rockhouse, fifty feet above the confluence of the two streams. It was dusk when Dull Knife stepped into its shelter and Jenny was allowed to sit down for the first real respite she had known since dawn. A warrior used flint and tiny splinters to kindle a fire. As others dragged in firewood, Jenny did not move. Black Wolf watched her with the measuring eye of a slave trader. Her child lay hot and unmoving at her breast. Tige sat staring at her, sympathy and worry etched in his round brown eyes.

Presently the old Shawnee took two short poles and leaned them against the face of the cliff in a remote corner of the rockhouse. He draped his buffalo robe over them to create a sheltered niche which he indicated was for Jenny's use. He broiled jerky for her and gave her handfuls of the hard parched corn, directing to her to eat it all.

The exhausted child had lost interest in food. Like her own his face was flushed, and his breath came in short, sucking gasps. Black Wolf, too, observed these symptoms. With a knife and hatchet he disappeared into the forest and soon returned with a handful of roots and bark which he washed in the swirling creek. These he boiled together for several minutes in a small iron pot. When the decoction had cooled he poured some of it into a terrapin-shell bowl. Squatting on his haunches he watched her drink it, then gestured to the child. The potion was black and extremely bitter. The child resisted to but eventually swallowed the equivalent of a dozen spoonfuls.

Black Wolf then stripped some bark from a small white-oak tree and boiled the inner layers in the same kettle. This time he directed Jenny to bathe her feet in the brew. To her immense gratification the swelling diminished and the torn and blistered heels were much soothed.

A hunting party returned with the gutted carcass of a black bear which was promptly skinned and its flesh distributed among the marauders. Black Wolf rendered some of the fat by cooking it in his pot. He poured the colorless and tasteless lard into the terrapin-shell bowl and handed it to Jenny. Grateful for the energy and strength she knew it to contain, she swallowed it with eagerness. Black Wolf refilled the shell and pointed with a slender copper-colored finger toward the child. The infant stirred and swallowed the liquid fat with the willingness and appetite he had previously reserved for milk.

The Indians commenced a feast that lasted several hours, but the medicine they had swallowed at the hands of the old Shawnee sent a warm glow of relaxation and sleepiness through their captives. The medicine man nodded toward the sleeping area behind the hide lean-to and gave her another animal skin for a covering. He promised that a share of the bear meat would be saved for their morning meal. Within the little shelter she cuddled the child to her bosom and felt him relax in sleep. She would never learn the nature of the medicine Black Wolf had prepared for her but she would always remember it as a boon, because under its influence she and the child slept the night away despite the tumult about them.

Again she was awakened at dawn to find Black Wolf

bending over her. The others were already stirring and the remainder of the bear meat was being broiled for their morning meal. She felt refreshed and her fever was much abated but she was measurably weaker and slower than when her ordeal began. Struggling to her feet, she repeated the treatment of her feet with the healing lotion brewed from the white-oak bark. She boiled out some of the bear fat and gave it to the child. True to his word, Black Wolf had saved a portion of the cooked meat from the night's feast and he handed it to her in the terrapin shell. It had been boiled without salt or other seasoning and was far from appetizing, but she ate it and gave morsels of it to the child. She rubbed his chest with the fat and poured down his throat some of the sleep-inducing brew the medicine man had cooked the night before. To soften the hard and cracked leather, she rubbed the rest of the bear fat onto her shoes.

Before they left camp the Indians carefully extinguished every trace of their camp and fire. With Dull Knife again in the lead and without evidence of discomfort or weariness ever appearing in the Indians, they climbed hills and crossed valleys, wading streams and traversing canebrakes and thickets. To her great relief, a Shawnee demeaned himself in the eyes of his companions by shouldering her baby for several hours. In taking the child from her arms, and later, when he abruptly handed him back to her, the warrior said nothing. She said a word or two in gratitude, the only utterances heard along the line of march for many hours. Again they ate a scanty noon meal of parched corn, rested briefly and plunged on to the northwest.

In the afternoon, as they passed through a gap between two valleys, the lookouts returned to report that a large party of heavily armed and mounted men were on their trail. They were making no effort to track their quarry but were moving rapidly along game paths. There were ten of them headed by Ski-goos-tee-ay himself. The scouts were visibly unsettled by the apparent ability of the whites to seek them out so quickly and unerringly and some of the warriors muttered of sorcery. It was clear that at the present rate they would be overtaken within hours and would have to fight for their captives and for their very lives.

This information brought dark and sullen looks down on the woman and child and inspired a heated debate. Dull Knife proposed that the child be killed at once and that they change the direction of their flight to due west. If the woman, relieved of the burden of her child, could keep up she would be retained as a captive. Otherwise, she, too, would die. Black Wolf approved the abrupt change of direction but urged that the child be spared, at least for the moment. The woman, he believed, could keep up, and in her anxiety to save her child would make a desperate effort to do so. Some of the braves proposed that Black Wolf and one other go ahead with the captives and effect an escape while the others prepared an ambush. Neither of the chiefs believed this proposal to have any chance of success. Even the Cherokee conceded that there was little hope of outwitting Tice Harman in this manner. All argument collapsed in a sudden agreement that a quickened flight to the west was the wisest course of action.

Jenny made an earnest little speech in English, intermingled with some of the Cherokee words he knew. She told them of her desire to save her only remaining child and promised to make every effort to keep pace with them. With much dignity, she asked that they spare her child, stating that he was strong and handsome and innocent in any wars between white men and red.

With a malevolent and wordless scowl Dull Knife shouldered his rifle and struck off. Two other braves were sent back as lookouts, and with hastening steps the warriors fled. Not without a little glow of satisfaction did Jenny note the obvious dread with which they struggled to elude a nemesis who sought them out through trackless forests and a bewildering maze of mountains.

CHAPTER SEVEN

They descended the mountain, walking in the bed of a small stream until the water became so deep they could no longer do so. Dull Knife then led them up another hillside to the left of their advance to the top of a ridge beetling with mountain laurel. Following its crest a short distance, they struggled down a steep rocky slope to another swirling stream which they pursued to its juncture with a much larger one. As they plowed ahead, Jenny's heart sank. She knew to a certainty that in her present condition she could not long carry the heavy child and maintain the pace set by the husky savages. Her pregnancy, the grief she had endured now for nearly seventy-two hours, the long marches across incredibly rough terrain, inadequate food and the weight of the child were combining to crush her. Perceptibly the band spread out. Dull Knife was far in advance, invisible at times to Jenny and Black Wolf. Twice those in front waited for the rear to catch up. The old Shawnee put Jenny in front of him and pushed her when she flagged. To make matters worse, the weather took an ominous turn. An unseasonable storm began building up directly before them in the west. A low rumble of thunder ran across the hilltops and lightning rippled along the horizon. The roar deepened and came more frequently. Tongues of fire swept through the heavens and the wind whistled through the trees, whipping leaves into rustling gales. As the discouraged woman struggled along the bank of the nameless stream, rain began pattering upon her head and face. In the deepening dusk, a great arc of lightning leaped across the heavens and by its flash she beheld a sight that chilled her heart. Approaching down the line of marching Indians came the Cherokee chief, his rifle slung across his shoulder in characteristic manner with the stock behind and his left hand grasping the muzzle, a determination in his gait and face that left no doubt of his intentions.

With a low sob she turned and dashed past Black Wolf, fleeing up the somber little valley. Both Black Wolf and Dull Knife sprang after her and within a few dozen yards the Shawnee seized her arm and whirled her about. A moment later the Cherokee, too, reached her side. She stood under the branches of a colossal beech, staring with parted lips and horrified eyes into the pitiless faces—the Shawnee's calm and inscrutable as always and the Cherokee's contorted with hate and anger.

The Cherokee's iron hands wrested the infant from her arms. He emitted a single piercing shriek, the same kind of heart-rending cry Jenny had heard from pigeons caught up in the clutches of a hawk. The little body whirred through the air and the pink, downy head smashed against the bole of the tree. The shriek ended with indescribable abruptness, then the keen scalping knife flashed around the shattered pate. Again she heard the stomach-churning sound of scalp parting from skull. The body was dropped amid the gnarled roots and the Indians hustled her toward their waiting fellows. They sped down the new stream, following a dim game trail by its banks. As they ran the great storm fell upon them with savage fury. Within seconds Jenny was soaked. The rain gushed from their garments but the downpour did not impede their flight. Presently above the noise of the storm Jenny heard the rush of a huge body of water and the creek they were following plunged into a swollen river—the stream known then and today as the Tug Fork of the Big Sandy. A moment later they gathered around Dull Knife, staring at the sullen avalanche of heaving gray water.

By the lightning Jenny saw that the stream was nearly fifty yards across and was running deep and swift. The water lapped against lower branches of sycamores and willows, and half-submerged logs and heaps of drift brush floated past.

A few words passed between the Indians but Jenny could not catch their meaning because they were drowned by the roar of thunder. New horror was piled upon her reeling senses when two of the strongest braves seized her on either side and dragged her into the rushing torrent. Her cry of protest died on her lips as the cold water swirled about her. Jenny was a strong swimmer, but shock and weariness almost proved too much for her. She thrashed about in the water and her head disappeared under the waves. The Indians pulled her up, but not before she had swallowed a mouthful of the flood. The warriors clung to her arms and, swimming in a curious upright manner, struck out onto the bosom of the stream. She heard low splashes as the other Indians followed them into the water.

The Indians did not push directly into the swift current but worked their way slowly across it, allowing themselves to drift with the flow of the river. Their rifles and powder horns were bound across the tops of their packs and they were impeded by their other gear. They swam in a clumsy fashion with their hands and shoulders out of the water, but their dexterity reminded Jenny of otters. They eluded the floating debris, and after the first shock of horror and cold a measure of Jenny's strength and resolve returned and she swam as her father had taught her years ago. Bit by bit they worked their way into the middle of the stream. Then slowly the far bank approached, but the struggle was desperate. Illuminated by lightning, rain drenched cliffs and trees spun before her eyes as the waters whirled them around like corks. As her own strength ebbed she sensed that the Indians at her side were weakening also. They panted and gasped and by perceptible degrees their grip on her arms relaxed. Other warriors, swimming unimpeded, passed them bobbing up and down on the tossing current. The water lapped against her mouth, a reddish mist gathered before her eyes and a low hum sounded in her ears. As a vast lethargy settled on her limbs, she felt the ground beneath her feet, and the braves staggered into the shoal water. Dragging her with them, they sank breathless in the shallow waters of a small stream flowing in from the west bank of the river.

For many minutes the Indians lay by Jenny's side breathing hard through parted lips. In her weariness she leaned against them and heard their hearts drumming beneath their soaked deerskin shirts.

When the warriors struggled to their feet, Jenny crawled after them on her hands and knees to the shore. One of them dragged her up the grassy bank and the diminishing lightning revealed the bedraggled marauders under the leafless branches of a huge sycamore. They sat or stood on a little grass-grown flat peering back across the river. Jenny's gaze followed theirs. A vast fork of fire flickered across the rainswept river and a final thunderclap rolled across the sky. Clearly revealed were a band of horsemen a scant hundred yards away. On the foremost horse, a gray stallion, sat a diminutive rain-drenched figure with a yellow beard. A long slender rifle lay across his saddle and his finger pointed toward the tree where the Indians rested. Then the lightning died. The departing thunder dwindled into a sigh and stygian darkness descended upon the gigantic forest.

The indefatigable Dull Knife resumed the westward trek. The hours dragged on in numbing dreariness. Jenny later remembered only bits and snatches of the night— wading streams, sloshing along their rocky beds for interminable periods, forcing her way through tangles of laurel, and, at one point, crawling in cold horror along the brink or a windswept precipice. Her system shrieked in protest against the perverse outrage to which her strength and sanity were subjected, but like an automaton in a nightmare she crept after her tormentors. Her disappointment and frustration were beyond measure. She had been so near to rescue and freedom, only to be whirled into a new maelstrom of agony and despair! More than once she considered a complete surrender—a collapse that was certain to bring down the tomahawks. But her will did not snap entirely, so that she murmured, "Not now! not now!" as she trudged through the deepening horror.

About two o'clock in the morning Black Wolf led them up a small stream to a narrow rockhouse. The place was magnificently hidden. The cliff was no more than four feet high and its entrance was screened by a dense tangle of laurel growing to the edge of the sandstone. A few pieces of firewood lay under the cliff, where, mercifully, it was dry. A modest blaze was started and the Indians gathered close around it for heat. All of them were ravenous, but the only food was the bag of parched corn, now thoroughly soaked. When they had eaten, all but two lay down and went to sleep. The two Wyandots went back to watch for Harman and his men.

This time Black Wolf took no chances on the possibility of escape. He bound Jenny's wrists and ankles with thongs, and as the Indians snored on each side of her the hide dried and bit into her flesh like cords of fire.

A combination of afflictions made this night truly hellish. The fire was small and she was soaked. The handful of parched corn had done little to allay her hunger. Her clothing hung in shreds, her hair was filthy and hopelessly tangled, and her hands and face were scratched and bloody. After the heavy downpour, the night was cold. She lay trussed under a buffalo skin, her teeth clicking, her mind black with despair and new grief. The murder and scalping of her child recurred endlessly before her. She became sick to her stomach and retched. As the thongs sank into her flesh, she fainted, but the blessed oblivion was short-lived. Soon she awoke to find Tige by her side licking her swollen hands. In her agony she cried out but the sleeping Indians did not stir. She struggled to her knees and crawled to the recumbent Black Wolf. She shook him and he sat up. For a long instant he stared at her, then examined her hands and ankles. He loosened the bonds and sat for several moments reflecting. Then he rebound her feet, but not as tightly as before. As an extra precaution he tied the end of the cord to his own wrist. Then without a word or backward glance he rolled up in his buffalo robe and resumed his slumbers.

Throughout the night, the little dog was her only link

to sanity as nightmare followed nightmare across her fitful sleep. An immense, warm and fetid serpent engulfed her in strangling folds. She fell from a vast height through a black and bottomless abyss. A mire of sinking quicksand pulled her down, suffocating and terrified, while Tom Wiley stood a few yards away unaware of her plight—and she was powerless to call to him or to make any sound. The psychic battering of these ghastly dreams was more overwhelming than the brutal realities that surrounded her when Black Wolf aroused her at dawn.

Dull Knife sat up and tossed a stone to awaken the warrior nearest him. Abruptly the camp stirred. Three of the warriors crept away and disappeared into the mist. As daylight came she heard a shot and the men returned carrying the carcass of a small deer. Quickly it was cut up and distributed. The fire was rekindled and the raw flesh was set on sticks to broil. The lookouts returned and joined them in a hurried meal. They reported to their companions in a low voice and at the far end of the cliff, outside Jenny's hearing. Their intelligence was consoling because the Indians relaxed somewhat and did not break camp until the last of the meat had been devoured. Jenny swallowed her share of the half-raw mess and scraps of the meat were tossed to the pup.

This day's march was more rugged than any other. They hiked in almost a straight line toward the southwest, aiming for a new fording place designated by the old Shawnee, clambering up one hill and scrambling down the next—ascending and descending again and again. The murder of her child doubtless saved her own life, because on this day his weight would have crushed her. As it was, she remained a great trial to Black Wolf, who growled impatiently when she paused for breath or wearily slowed her steps. They followed dim paths, struggled through trailless thickets up boulder-strewn hillsides, and skirted perpendicular cliffs. Late in the day they came to another flood-swollen river— a stream known to Harman and other long hunters as the Louisa River and later known as the Levisa—the name it bears today. It, too, carried much driftwood, leaves and heaps of uprooted cane. They rested for a half-hour. Then Dull Knife stood up, bound his pack high on his shoulder, and tied his rifle and powder horn on top of it. With a disdainful toss of his head and a gloomy scowl he stepped into the water and began to swim. Again the two Wyandots seized Jenny and pulled her into the river. The crossing was fully as formidable as the previous night's. Several times they swam until their strength was exhausted, then drifted with the cold water until they were in some measure rested. It was a disconsolate band that finally emerged on the western bank.

After a breathing spell the Indians followed a small stream for a half-mile or so, then ascended a hill to its crest. This they followed to the north for a few hundred yards, and descended a faint trail on the western side. An hour after nightfall found them at the edge of a well-hidden cliff. The entrance was low, so that in entering it Jenny had to crawl on her hands and knees. Once within, however, the roof rose nearly a dozen feet. A thicket of scrub pine grew close about the entrance and screened the fire they quickly lighted. This night the last of the parched corn was eaten, and without posting lookouts the Indians curled up around the fire and slept. It was evident that they did not take seriously the idea that Jenny could now escape or that Harman and his searchers could find them. She was not bound and, though she was hungry and her taut nerves ached from weariness and strain, she fell into a slumber that lasted until long after daylight. When she opened her eyes, most of the warriors had already risen, but several slept. The absent ones, she knew, were hunting and would soon return with game. When she emerged she found Black Wolf sitting in the October sunlight smoking a clay pipe stuffed with willow bark and tobacco, an expression of benign calm on his wrinkled face. The flight had ended. Tice Harman's attempt to rescue her and to punish her abductors had failed. Jenny's hope for freedom had been long—perhaps permanently—deferred.

CHAPTER EIGHT

Within an hour after Jenny awakened, the hunters returned carrying the hindquarters of a buffalo cow. Others went out and brought back other parts of the carcass. Black Wolf directed Jenny to gather firewood and she dragged in an immense heap of fallen branches.

The lookouts came in from the east, and from their general unconcern it was clear that the pursuit had ended. From the aspect of the land Jenny surmised that she had been carried into that vast intricate tangle of steep slopes and tumbling creeks known to hunters as the Kaintucke Mountains. While she traversed the headwaters of the Bluestone and later, when they moved westward toward the Tug, she had been buoyed by a slender hope that Harman, her husband and their neighbors would overtake them. Now that hope was extinguished.

The eastern third of Kentucky, Virginia's immense western country, was a labyrinth of 15,000 square miles. It lay between the Great or Big Sandy and its tributaries on the east and the rolling meadows of the central plain on the west—a country as large as Switzerland without a single white inhabitant. The only people who moved within its fastnesses were occasional white hunters and bands of marauding Indians passing between the villages in Tennessee and Ohio. This was the very heart of Appalachia, where scarcely a tree had been cut in all the ages since the first human foot touched its soil. Major war trails followed its three main river valleys and ancient game traces laced the region. There were dim paths on the hill, followed occasionally by bands of Indians and by wild animals, but these trails were scarcely visible except to the eyes of experienced woodsmen. For white men, however resourceful and determined, to seek out a handful of Indians in such territory was much more difficult than finding a needle in a haystack. The needle was made virtually unfindable by its ability to move, to reason and to obliterate all signs of its passing. None of these harsh facts was lost on the weary woman.

Footsore and nerve-wracked, Jenny struggled to find strength to gather the fuel. The day was crisp and despite the chill she had to go about her task barefooted. Her torn and blistered feet could no longer endure contact with her shoes. Black Wolf saw her plight and brewed more of the lotion from the white-oak bark, and again she felt prompt improvement. Again she drank the strange black, bitter "medicine" that he had boiled from roots and bark. Under its warmth, she felt the cold and fever dying in her lungs and blood.

As the pile of wood grew, the Indians prepared to cook the meat. A pit was dug, wood was burned, and the pit was filled with hot coals. The raw flesh was placed in the half-filled hole and was covered by other layers of coals. The heat was maintained for several hours and in this manner a prodigious amount of the buffalo was roasted.

Confident though they were, the Indians did not let their guard down entirely. A brave ate some of the meat and slipped away toward the river to watch for a possible crossing by the unpredictable Harman. The others began to eat, squatting on their haunches around the fire, their buttocks scant inches above the sandy earth. They held the roasted meat in their greasy fingers or by sharp sticks with which they pierced the chunks. Slowly, relentlessly, they consumed the huge heap of charred "beef." They had been on the trail for a long time with too little food and now they gorged like famished wolves on the carcass of their prey.

Jenny was extremely faint from sustained hunger. During the last forty-eight hours she had eaten nothing except a few handfuls of parched corn and scanty bits of venison. Notwithstanding their famine and her own Jenny was astounded by the amount of meat they consumed. Pound by pound the carcass vanished.

She was allowed to eat all she wanted, but it had been cooked without salt. Seeing her distaste for it, Black Wolf poured about a spoonful of the mineral into her hand. She sprinkled it on her food, an action the Indians viewed with obvious disgust. The seasoning added immensely to her enjoyment of the meal and the food gave her a surge of new strength.

After the warriors had gorged themselves they flung their buffalo robes about their shoulders and crept into the cave to sleep. They lay in a circle with their feet toward the center. When all had gone except Jenny and Black Wolf, he studied her suspiciously, his eyes narrowed to thin slits. He puffed his pipe in silence for several minutes, then took a tomahawk and stuck it deep into the earth in a unmistakable gesture. "If white squaw try to run away," he said, "white squaw die!" Then he, too disappeared into the hidden grotto.

Jenny took quick advantage of the marvelous period of privacy. Two hundred yards up the stream she found a deep basin filled with cold rushing water. Removing her clothing, she stepped into it. Her body was filthy with dried sweat and blood, and dirt and smoke from many campfires. The October air bit her flesh as she scooped up handfuls of the white sand from the bottom and rubbed it into her hair, using it as an abrasive to clean her locks and scalp. She rubbed her face and entire body with the same rough cleanser. She finished by scouring her tortured feet and found the return to cleanliness delightfully rejuvenating.

She then scrubbed her clothing in the same manner. Her outer garments were little more than shreds, ripped by briars and branches and countless falls on rocks and logs. She hung them on tree branches to dry in the wind and weak autumn sun.

When she had dressed again she realized that she could not go much farther in her clumsy shoes. Dried our from their many soakings, the leather was almost as stiff as a board. She would have to have moccasins, and as a daughter of the frontier, she knew how to make them.

At sunset when Black Wolf crawled out of the cave he was visibly pleased by the transformation of his white captive. She had combed her hair with a turkey feather and had bound it behind her head in a tight roll. The old medicine man looked at her bare feet, then brought a roll of deerskin from his pack. Jenny had worn the soft Indian footgear much of each year and had made many pairs for her own and her children's feet, but Black Wolf did not give the leather to her. Instead he measured her feet and went to work with awl and needle. In a village, with motivation and plenty of time, he could have produced beaded and beautifully decorated moccasins; but for the present, utility was the only object. Within little more than an hour, the primitive shoes were finished. Jenny put them on and bound them securely in place with scraps of leather. In them she could walk much more easily and surely than had previously been possible.

Through all the next day the Indians slept or lounged about the campfire, sometimes smoking for hours while gazing silently at the blazing embers. They reminded the woman of resting dogs after a long and arduous chase.

Dull Knife used the occasion to stretch the scalps of his victims on loops of willow and dry them to parchment by the smoky fire. The spectacle of the gruesome trophies bouncing in the ascending air currents pierced her with irresistible anguish and bitterness. She crept away to a sunny little clearing by the creek and there, at last, permitted tears to wash away a measure of her despair. The tears flowed for a bereavement, a loss, a frustration so overwhelming as to threaten to swamp her sanity: for her children and brother dead; for the agonizing and horror-filled way of their dying; for the years of love and achievement lost to them, their children and their get forever; for Tom Wiley—good, generous, kind and brave—and the shattered center, foundation and purpose of his life; for the termination of the dreams she and her mate had launched in a wilderness clearing; and last, and least, for the hopeless frightfulness of her own captivity and slavery. But the tears healed a little and the hour-long session with her grief-torn soul brought her a new sense of calm and fortitude and cleared her mind to a steadier comprehension of the stern self-duty which alone could ever set her free.

The Indians used a portion of the time to take their rifles apart and clean them carefully. The metal was rubbed dry and coated with bear grease. The priceless firearms were treated better then any other possessions of which the savages could boast. They also examined the contents of the tightly stoppered powder horns and noted with satisfaction that the corned black powder had come through without dampening.

Tige trailed her like a shadow. He slept near her at night in a corner of the rockhouse. None of the Indians resented his presence and occasionally patted him or rubbed his head and ears.

The rest was a godsend to Jenny. Without the two days at the camp, the plentiful food and the opportunity to bathe she could have gone no farther. Even so, when the march was resumed before daybreak on the third day, her strength was far depleted. But now the Indians moved at a leisurely rate. They stopped at frequent intervals to find nuts or hunt for succulent small game.

Though her flesh was allowed a measure of respite, the essential horror of her situation was unabated. The mere presence of the Cherokee chief sent chills of dread down her spine. The eyes that sometimes sought her face mirrored hatred, malevolence, and frustration. They reflected, also, an essential outlaw quality, a basic perverseness that set him apart from all society, whether red or white. A subtle intuition warned her that Dull Knife's cruelty might mask his admiration and lust for her.

When sunlight gleamed on his silver adornments or his footfall rustled the leaves near her side she was seized by a new apprehension for the day when her child was born. Then she would be eligible for both adoption and marriage—

a lifetime of double damnation as both slave and harlot. Her spirit quailed before the grim possibilities that lay in wait for her, and the shadow of Dull Knife towered darkly in her fears.

And increasingly she was disturbed by twinges of pain. Though she was but seven months advanced, the battering ordeals through which she had passed would certainly shorten her time. The consequences of premature child birth were not pleasant to contemplate. Weakened by her ordeal, she feared that neither she nor her soon-to-be-born child could possibly survive the remainder of the journey.

Sometimes they followed the broad game trail by the riverbank and, at others, walked the hills overlooking the stream. From a crag she looked down on the confluence of the Tug and Levisa Forks and to the broadened valley beyond through which coiled the river of mystery.

In the cane by the river, they saw herds of deer, and at a broad shallow ford, hundreds of buffalo stood dark and majestic, clad in thick new coats for the winter. An ancient bull bellowed his displeasure at their passing, his head lowered in imperishable dignity, his voice hoarse with challenge. She would always remember the melancholy sound of the water mingled with the bawling of cows and calves. That night they camped nearby and again feasted on roasted buffalo meat.

A day's march above the river junction, they came to the Painted Licks. Long before she was captured, Jenny had heard them described by returning hunters, but the color, the barbaric splendor and the almost infinite number of the paintings amazed her.

The first painting they encountered was on a sycamore. The bark had been stripped away, baring the smooth, white wood for six feet above the ground. The huge bole was encircled with figures in red and black. Men, buffalo, bear, birds and serpents followed each other about the column, interspersed with mystic devices—swastika, circles and curious beanlike shapes. Thereafter such trees were found with increasing frequency. Eventually, they broke out onto a broad river bottom. From the west a stream flowed in, and as far as she could see in all directions there were dead and barren trees decorated in a staggering profusion of weird and fantastic designs. One huge poplar had been painted to a prodigious height. Many had fallen, with splotches of the ancient color surviving on the rotted trunks.

Rocky ledges bore the same designs, always in red and black and always the same stiff, sticklike outlines of men, animals, fish and fowls intermingled with the incomprehensible stylized symbols.

Here and there were bubbling springs, the earth packed hard and barren for many acres about them and carpeted with enormous accumulations of manure and bones. These were the salt licks, the saline springs which had attracted untold generations of animals and the men and beasts that preyed upon them.

To the west, smooth low hills rose out of the river bottom. One attained a height of fifty feet and in outline resembled a huge inverted saucer. Trees grew on its slopes. Beyond it were many smaller mounds, some only fifty or sixty feet in diameter, and more sharply sloping on their sides. These were man-made hills, piled in the dim past, though for what purpose neither she nor any other people at that time could surmise.

Eastward, beyond the Louisa, a long, low curving ridge bordered the river and along its crest stood a row of rotted cabins. The roofs had fallen in and the chimneys were collapsing under the weight of wild grapevines. A tall young hickory had grown up through a broken and rotted wall. She judged the cabins to be older than old Henry Harman himself—the work of long-dead French fur traders whose yearning for profit had sent them into this wilderness generations before the first English-speaking long hunter.

At the Painted Licks a marked change came over the savages. The occasional banter and gaiety of the young warriors vanished. They fell into a solemn mood, passing in utter silence along the shadowy trail. When they came opposite the great mound Black Wolf signaled a halt. Standing a hundred yards east of its slopes, he laid aside his pack and deerskin jacket. Stripping to the skin from the waist up he faced the mound and stretched his arms toward it. For a long silent moment he stood in this pose and then began a low monotonous singsong chant. Clearly, the ancient landmark was of age-old religious significance—a symbol of departed glories and generations of reverence. Nuns in a Spanish cathedral could have displayed no more awe or wonder than the pitiless Dull Knife at this antique monument. The hard lines of his face softened and his bitter frown relaxed into solemnity and, for a moment, peace.

Before leaving the Licks the Indians stripped the bark from one side of a young birch and two of them mixed paints from some sort of ingredients they carried in their packs. Fine powders were sprinkled into water and stirred to a paste. Two colors—red and black—were prepared. Using their fingers they traced outlines similar to those that they had passed. There emerged from their fingertips red men and black, a red buffalo, a black bear, a long red serpent, strange elongated swastikas and the beanlike shape. Then, with a few deft strokes, one painted a beanpole caricature of a human being. It was a woman, and the slatlike form was arrayed in distinctive garments—the skirts and bodice of a white squaw.

When the Painted Licks were behind them the Indians began to find their tongues again. Jenny used some of the Shawnee words she had acquired to ask Black Wolf whether his people had built the strange mound. Black Wolf was obviously pleased by her interest. When he stopped and gazed back up the valley toward the gaudy signposts he shrugged his shoulder and answered with a mystifying declaration that the mounds were full of fire and death.

In their references to the valley and the licks the Indians used many times the tongue-twisting term "Mich-e-cho-be-ka-sepe." From her growing accumulation of both Cherokee and Shawnee words and her memories of conversations with Cherokee Jim she grasped its meaning—the Valley of Big Medicine or the Valley of Mystery. And it was not unaptly named—the tree-clad hills, the vast fields of wild cane, the surging river, the wild creatures, the weird columns with their messages of war and death and, over all, a brooding expectant hush that had endured since the beginning of time.

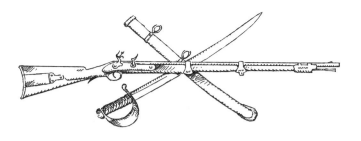

CHAPTER NINE

The rain drummed relentlessly against the whiteoak roof boards of John Border's cabin. Like all people of the frontier, Elizabeth and John Borders lived uneasily, but they had disciplined their nerves and steeled their souls against panic, to stand in the face of danger and choke off the impulse to flee or to "fort up" behind cabin walls. On this evening Borders could point to nothing very definite for the cause of his dread. He felt a bit sheepish, even silly, on the matter of the owl hoots—after all, the probability was overwhelming that the sounds were genuine. In his persistent consideration of the matter he had told himself over and over that the cries had sounded authentic in every respect. Still, the dread lingered and as the night darkened he suddenly resolved to have Jenny and her household under his roof without further delay.

Taking down the Brown Bess flintlock musket that hung clean and dry above the leaping flames of the fireplace, he carefully checked its priming. It was loaded with a massive charge of powder behind a handful of iron and lead slugs. He buckled on a keen homemade sword and, bidding his wife goodbye, stepped into the darkness. Before he passed through the door he urged her to spread pallets on the floor for Jenny and her children and to keep a big fire going. They would be wet when they arrived and in sore need of a dry room and warm beds. Without them they might catch severe colds, and a cold on the frontier was a serious matter—often leading to pneumonia and the grave.

Borders was not adept at Indian warfare. Neither his life in the Old World nor his military training had prepared him for it, and his sojourn in the backwoods was only five years old. But he had learned a great deal. He had a keener instinct for the backwoods life than did his brother-in-law. Tom Wiley was a farmer. Every breeze he sniffed, everything he touched or tasted was related immediately in his mind to farming—to plowing, to planting, to the seasons. He hunted only when his table needed the meat. Borders, by contrast, like the chase and as time passed he spent more and more time in the hills looking for deer or bear, or simply sitting on some rocky pinnacle soaking in the majesty and magnificence of the forest. The sweeping wild backwoods grew in this manner on most men who came to them, converting many of them into "woods runners"—hunters and wanderers who were, in the eyes of settled farmers, mere idle vagabonds. The wilderness had begun to get a grip on John Borders. In addition, he was a brave man who detested Indians without fearing them. To Borders, their stealthy hit-and-run tactics, their obscene tortures, their willingness to fight and flee and return to strike again, were cowardly and thoroughly contemptible. But he was developing a grudging respect for them as adversaries, and a deepening comprehension of the patience that so often accompanied impetuosity when they set out for scalps and booty.

Thus, on this occasion, he took with him neither dogs nor lantern. He moved silently along the trail, protecting his musket's frizzen, pan and flint with a piece of heavy, greased leather. Passing over the ridge above the Wiley house, he saw a spectacle that chilled him and hastened his footsteps while increasing his caution.

The cabin was afire, the flames leaping through the roof and casting a flickering light for a score of yards around it. From the ridgetop he carefully surveyed the land about the burning structure for signs of savages, but saw none. As he approached, the downpour quickened and amid much hissing and a cascading of sparks the fire dwindled and died. Borders stopped in the shadows of some trees, and stood watching and listening for several moments. Presently Wiley's dogs came out of the hills to the west and sniffed about the cabin, obviously puzzled by the destruction that had been wrought during their absence. When they discovered Borders, they barked ferociously until his identity was ascertained, then slunk back into the darkness.

When he was convinced that Indians were not lying in ambush about the place he went to the door. The roof had fallen and the droning rain was extinguishing the burning brands. The shattered door lay where it had fallen. A low rumble of thunder rolled hollowly in the west and a long flicker of lightning leaped above the valley. Tables, chairs and broken fragments of beds had been piled in the middle of the floor and set afire. The leaping flames had burned out the loft and roof and had eaten through the puncheon floor. However, the blackened walls appeared little damaged. Feathers from pillows lay white and sodden everywhere.

Sputtering brands dropping from the roof revealed the ghastly fate of the Wiley household. Jenny's half-brother lay near the hearth, his head caved in, blood streaming across the huge flat stone. Around him in grotesque positions lay the dead bodies of the Wiley children—all of them except the baby. Pushing in, he saw the cradle was empty. There was no trace of the infant or his mother. He called for them but there was no sound except the rain and the sizzling of the hot embers. Going outside he searched for them over a radius of a hundred yards or more. From the beginning he recognized the almost certain fate of the young woman and her baby: they had been carried into captivity—probably to the south in the villages of the Cherokee.

Rapidly retracing his steps to his own cabin, he told the horrified Elizabeth of the atrocity he had discovered. Though she wept for her brother, her sister and her sister's children, this daughter of Hezekiah Sellards wept through gritted teeth. As Borders left to carry the alarm to the widely scattered cabins, both he and his wife feared an attack would be launched against their own door long before he could return. As Elizabeth dropped the bar behind him she barricaded the portal with additional timbers and armed herself with the weapon so often wielded to such deadly effect by backwoods women—a long-handled, well-honed axe. While her frightened children huddled by the fire she listened for the barking of dogs to warn her of approaching danger.

Within two hours a considerable group had gathered at Tom Wiley's cabin to see the results of the Indian raid and to plan a rescue effort. In the absence of the Harman brothers, John and Henry Skaggs and most of the other experienced trackers, the settlers were bewildered and hesitant. The hunters were not expected to return for another week and many men still in the settlement were newcomers from the coast or Europe and the merest novices at tracking. Too, the best firearms had been carried away by the hunters. Tom Wiley himself would not get back until midnight or later. Nevertheless, a dozen determined men and youths were soon ready for the trail.

John Borders, Sam Wiley, Jenny's brothers Tom and Jack, Lazarus Damron, Absalom Lusk and six boys of sixteen or more armed themselves with knives and rifles and shouldered packs filled with smoked meat and parched corn. They were prepared to go in search of the missing woman and her baby as soon as daylight would allow them to find some evidence of the direction the raiders had followed.

And while they awaited the gray light of dawn the men carried the bodies of the dead across the hill to the Borders place. After the frontier fashion, friends and relatives washed the corpses and laid them out for burial. Pursuit would require several days, however it turned out, and the bodies would have to be interred in Tom Wiley's absence. During the coming day neighbors would dig the graves and fashion rude coffins. Coffins were generally carved out of poplar logs, and because death was a constant companion of the backwoods people, many families kept one or more on hand stored in a barn loft or corn shed.

In the droning rain John and Elizabeth Borders rode down the trail to meet their brother-in-law. After midnight they heard the sloshing of hooves against the muddy trail, and waiting patently, saw the black forms of a horse and rider emerge from the shadows of a buckeye. Elizabeth called Tom in a low plaintive voice. The shadow froze. "Liz!" he demanded. "Is that you? What are you doing out here on a night like this?" The hooves clumped again as the dripping horses and their riders faced each other in the darkness.

"What's wrong, Liz? John, what's the matter?" The voice was husky now, and pleading.

Elizabeth began to sob. "Tom," John Borders said in tones kept low and deep in order to keep them level, "Indians have been here. They've carried away Jenny and your baby. Your other children and Andrew are dead."

Tom Wiley was a steady, dependable man, of a calm disposition but capable of intense feeling. He sat in the saddle in silence for a long time, grieving deeply and assessing the immensity of the catastrophe that had befallen him and his household. "When did it happen?" was his first question. Briefly, Borders told him the circumstances. He described his visit to the doomed cabin that afternoon, his suspicions of the hooting owls, and his return two hours after darkfall. After another interval of silence Wiley said, "Let's go and see if we can find anything to show us which way they took her. What do you think, John? Did they take her north, or did they go south?"

Borders could only venture an opinion. In their sojourn in the valley they had rarely seen a Shawnee. They were reputed to come up the Big Sandy on hunting forays, spending the winters in towns north of the Ohio. He knew, as Wiley did, that they often visited the Cherokee to the south. But the little settlement had had many more contacts with the Cherokee and their kinsmen. In peaceful intervals, the southern Indians, including occasional Choctaws, Chickasaws and Creeks, had passed through the valley. Sometimes they stole cattle and horses grazing in the forest. "Big Jim," the Cherokee, had spent many nights in the settlement, some of them with Tom and Jenny Wiley. Because they had more knowledge of these southern tribes, it was natural that they concluded the marauders had come up from the Tennessee.

"If Tice Harman was here,"Borders said, "he could pick up the trail and tell us where they've gone. John Skaggs or Henry could do it, and some of the other men. But me and you, Tom, are pretty blind when it comes to trackin'. Some of these boys who have lived here nigh all their lives are tolerably good at it. When mornin' comes some of us might be able to pick up a trail, but I doubt it. I think we're goin' to have to just reason it out the best we can and try to decide where the devils come from. And it's my thinkin', for what it may be worth, that they've gone across the mountains and along the New River to the towns in the Tennessee country. And if I'm right about it, and if they don't lose their temper and kill her or the baby before they get there, your woman will be put up for ransom one of these times. They may keep the baby and bring him up an Indian. You know, Tom, it's happened many a time before. Harman tells about the times he's been to the Indian towns and seen a-plenty of whites and half-breeds."

Elizabeth choked on her tears and shook with the cold and dampness. "Everything's agin her," she said. "Even if they feed her and treat her fairly well, this cold rain will make her sick. It'll be a wonder if she comes through a night like this alive."

At the Borders cabin Wiley lighted a bear-grease candle and went to see the bodies of his murdered children and brother-in-law. They lay under rough homemade sheets. One by one he lifted the covering cloths and looked at the faces beneath the bloody, hairless skulls. Shaking with dry sobs, he left the shed where the bodies lay, and waited until dawn by the sputtering fire.

At daylight, the rescue party assembled at the

fireblackened cabin. The rain had stopped, but the night-long downpour had left the soil as soggy as a wet sponge and had washed out all tracks. Finding no footprints to indicate the direction taken by the fugitives Tom Wiley accepted the reasoning advanced by Borders and the party headed south across Walker's Mountain to the New River. They would forge ahead as rapidly as the stamina of their mounts would permit, hoping to overhaul the savages before they reached the headwaters of the New and disappear into the tangled steeps of the Iron Mountains—some of which soared almost to six thousand feet. The Indians would be burdened by a pregnant woman struggling to carry a year-old child. Perhaps they would assume that since the rain had washed out their tracks they could not be followed and, in consequence, become overconfident. The pursuers prayed that their quarry would dawdle along the trail, for therein lay their only hope of success.

The little band was in decisive error on another point also. They believed the red culprits numbered no more than three or four. It was reasoned that a larger party would have attacked other cabins. They concluded that a few warriors had passed through the valley and had broken into the lonely cabin on impulse. Laden with spoils and captives, they had headed for their villages by the most direct route—destinations some two hundred miles to the south and west. Once in those high fastnesses there was little real hope of getting them out again. No army then in existence on the North American continent could fight its way into the heartland of the Cherokee nation.

The pursuers moved with considerable confidence. They anticipated that they would outnumber the savages and hoped to find them in camp. With luck and daring, a volley of well-aimed shots would kill or disable Jenny's captors and assure her recovery unharmed. They were chilled by the tendency of Indians to massacre prisoners when attacked, and the possibility that they would recover only two more mutilated bodies was a real one that had to be faced steadily and calmly.

Tom Wiley was tragically shaken and weakened. He had had no sleep during the preceding night, and had arrived home soaked to the skin. Wholly without appetite, he forced himself to eat a substantial breakfast before setting out on the trail. Of gentle and diligent instincts, he was known widely for his kindliness and affability. Since his marriage his interests had centered closely around his wife and children and his farm, so that some of the men in the settlement—those given to long hunts and robust backwoods merrymaking—had considered him to be aloof and even unfriendly. Now he was benumbed by grief for the dead and, simultaneously, was distracted by anxiety for his missing wife and child. He struggled manfully to keep command of his mind and nerves by an exercise of sheer will but despite his exertions found himself lost in an almost unconscious reverie for moments at a time. Of necessity, Borders assumed much of the responsibility for guiding the party.

All day they forced their way through the mountains, leading their horses up many slopes that were incredibly steep and little more than barren rock. Borders went ahead as a scout. They stopped for a five- or ten-minute break every hour. Their horses had foraged in the forest for several months and were not in prime condition. Now each carried thirty or forty pounds of grain in addition to a saddle. When ridden over the wild tumbling slopes of Walker's Mountain they tired quickly and had to be rested at regular and frequent intervals.

Even so, the hope of overtaking the Indians was not an unrealistic one. Once over the mountain, in the New River Valley, their pace quickened and the men and youths were heartened. They moved confidently and faster than even unencumbered braves could move on foot. In midafternoon, they were buoyed up by a conviction that if the marauders followed the southern trail that skirted the river to its headwaters they would overtake them by nightfall on the following day.

However, at the end of the day when the sun set and a chill darkness fell over the weary band, a general discouragement settled upon them. They had seen neither Indians nor any sign of them—not a moccasin print or broken twig or scuffed pebble to indicate that humans had preceded them on the trail. They built a fire and ate, and wrapping themselves in heavy blankets fell asleep—all except John Borders and Tom Wiley. Borders served as sentinel for the first part of the night, his Brown Bess across his knees. After forcing down a few mouthfuls of parched corn and broiled meat, Wiley tried to sleep. but despite his physical and spiritual fatigue, slumber would not come. The anguish that burned in his breast was too intense, his tears too near the surface. The night was a hellish torture. Crushing as was his grief for the mutilated bodies he had left behind, the anxiety he endured now for his wife and infant was vastly greater. It tore at his heart like steel tongs. A savage might crush his beloved, his affectionate, his incomparable Jenny at any moment—and such a fate might indeed be the most merciful she could covet. Unless he and his companions succeeded somehow in finding her soon, she would be lost to him, probably forever. The thought of his children's mother bound in unholy union to a painted savage, great with his child and tending his fire as both slave and harlot, caused him to bite his lip in a paroxysm of despair and frustration. More than once he pounded his forehead and groaned with an agony that would have welcomed death as a release from a dilemma that could be neither surmounted nor escaped. Not until the first streaks of dawn were in the sky was he able to find any peace. Then he fell into an unconsciousness induced by exhaustion and unbearable nervous tension, but his rest lasted only an hour or two. When the men stirred at dawn he awakened with a hot sickness at the pit of his stomach and his legs trembled beneath him as he struggled to rise.

Men and horses ate hurriedly, then pushed on. This day Wiley would not let them rest. Frantic in his desperation, he seemed to have conquered weariness. Somewhere he tapped a new and seemingly endless source of strength. But neither strength or desperation was enough, for long before the day's end it was apparent that they were going in the wrong direction. If human feet had traversed the ancient trace at any time within the last several weeks, they had left no intelligible marks. At sundown, a cold drizzle soaked the dispirited and hungry men and their equally disconsolate mounts. Near the upper reaches of the New River, where the stream babbled over a thousand yards of smooth round stones, under the shadows of towering peaks, Wiley and Borders called a halt. They found a rockhouse, well shielded by close-growing hemlocks, and managed to find enough dry wood to start a fire. When morning came, the band started the dreary trek back to the settlement.

The return was slower than the headlong rush into the wilderness. The horses were jaded, but Wiley pushed men and animals alike unrelentingly. He was determined to get back to Walker's Creek, organize a new rescue party and head toward the north. He was certain, now, that the Indians had gone toward the Big Sandy. Somewhere in the fastnesses of the western forest his wife might still live, nursing her baby and hoping against hope for rescue. The vision of his wife dragged through the forest by sullen and feather-decked savages renewed his strength each time it flagged. Long after midnight on the morning of October 5 they reached the southernmost cabin in the little settlement, and the tired and baffled men scattered to their homes.

Elizabeth Borders had barricaded the door of her house with heavy walnut fence rails in addition to the oak bar. The barking of dogs aroused her, and when she knew the identity of the men who called to her she struggled to remove the bar and braces.

As they entered the huge firelit room, Wiley presented a pathetic figure. Usually clean-shaven, his face was dark with a five-day growth of beard. His cheeks were sunken, his eyes were bloodshot, his shoulders sagged. Suddenly he seemed shriveled and old and spent.

CHAPTER TEN

The hunters' return to the Walker's Creek settlement was a harrowing one. Old Henry Harman's wounds were extremely painful and he was so weak from suffering and loss of blood that he was unable to ride alone. He was lifted onto the largest horse available, and Tice Harman, the smallest of the men, rode behind him to hold him in the saddle. Constant vigilance had to be maintained against the threat of ambush. The likelihood that the vengeful savages would head straight for the unprotected cabins could not wholly rule out the possibility that they could lie in wait in a canebrake or behind close growing trees.

However, a few hours on the trail convinced the hunters that their anxiety was largely needless. The game trace betrayed no mark of the passage of Indians. It was deepworn and broad—in places five or six feet across. A scuffing moccasin, a stumble, a lingering print on a miry clay would signal to keen eyes that men had preceded them. Intent study of such marks—their depth and age, the absence or accumulation of leaves and other trail debris upon them— would point to the number of persons and the direction pursued. But no such spoor were discovered and the men were bolstered in their conclusion that the raiders were following obscure paths and shortcuts though the mountains.

Tice Harman believed they could cross the Tug Fork of the Great Sandy and climb the Big Guyandotte ridge which runs generally northwest from the upper reaches of the Bluestone to the mouth of the Guyandotte River. They would follow the broad crest of the ridge to its terminus in the south, then cross the intervening ridges to Walker's Creek. An ancient trace marked that route and much of the way was across the Big Flat Tops, plateaus where travel was easy and venison abundant. But to reach it, the raiders would have to ford the Tug and its tributaries, no easy tasks because of the "drift tides" then running from heavy rains. Men on horseback could move much more swiftly. All things considered, the hunters could beat their enemies to their destination if no bad luck beset them.

But the Indians gained several hours' lead because the dressing of wounds and the breaking of camp proved to be time-consuming ordeals. The widely scattered horses and mules had to be rounded up and led back to the camp. More than five hours passed before they headed southward, pushing the animals hard to make up for the lost time.

The bleeding patriarch soon brought them to a halt. He had to be taken from the saddle and allowed to rest lying down. Robert Hawes, too, proved a problem. The ball had been withdrawn from his elbow by an operation, made unavoidable by the threat of gangrene, which caused him excruciating agony. He rode with his teeth clamped hard together on a stick to stifle his groans, and his misery mounted under the patient plodding of his mount. Both he and Harman became feverish and the party was forced into camp an hour after nightfall. The wounded men tumbled and groaned through much of the night. Hawes got no sleep. Eventually, the remarkable old Prussian drifted off, and toward dawn he was snoring sonorously. When he awoke he was much weakened, and all day long Tice held him in the saddle.

This was no easy task, despite the lightness of the old man's body. The trail skirted boulders, forded and reforded streams, wound up precipitous and rocky slopes, and skirted mist-shrouded crags. It threaded through cathedrals of immense trees and, almost invisible, crawled like a serpent through tangles of rhododendron and laurel. Such thickets closed in so tightly that the riders had to lead their horses and mules carefully along the shadowy tunnels while his sons carried Harman on a crude litter. The day was disappointing and the men swore with impatience as night drew on.

The gallon whiskey jug afforded the only surcease and the three wounded men were allowed to drink copiously as long as the spirits lasted. Hawe's arm became swollen and inflamed and sometimes he murmured incoherently. It became necessary for one of the men to ride with him, also. Thus the caravan was held to the slow pace of the two overloaded mounts.

After a night and two days on the trail, they came to the crest of the long, rocky ridge overlooking Walker's Valley. As dusk came on, they did not pause despite the groans of the wounded and a well-founded fear that continued exertions might kill old Harman. Through a cold, relentless rain they led their horses, their bodies clammy in soaked and clinging leather garments. Cursing as they crashed into trees and stumbled over stones and crevices, they toiled to cover the last miles, but despite herculean efforts the rain had ended and the sun had risen on a clear, crisp new day before they approached the first cabin in the settlement.

Because of the red man's habit of carefully scouting a target before assaulting it, all of them except Harman were confident they had outrun their foes. Harman's long experience in Indian warfare had taught him that when they were on the warpath the aborigines were practically tireless, that they could travel by day and night for incredible distances and that a lust for vengeance could motivate them to unbelievable feats. At dusk, as they filed down the last mountain, he feared the worst.

The mean little shelter that was Harman's place was on a narrow branch of Walker's Creek. It was the southernmost of all the habitations and the most isolated. Harman liked it that way and had built in the shelter of a little cove with a huge crag towering above it and jutting defiantly outward like the prow of a ship plowing through a sea of treetops. And since Tice Harman was a hunter and wanderer who hated the very thought of toil in any fixed place, his was the shabbiest cabin in the settlement, his fields the smallest and least carefully tilled. But it was with him that the old man made his habitation and they deposited him on a crude corded bed in the drab one-room shelter.

Before the octogenarian could be lifted from the saddle, Harman's wife told him of the murder of Tom Wiley's children and brother-in-law and the abduction of his wife and baby. The short-tempered borderer threw his huge, broad-brimmed hat on the ground and kicked it with vexation and rage, while swearing with wonderful asperity. He was not amazed that the raid had been made, but only that it had stopped with the destruction of a single family. He marveled that the savages had not attacked the others one by one until most of the settlement was obliterated.

The tormented Robert Haws was sent to his home and a council was held as to the best means of punishing the Indians and liberating their captives. The savages had struck nearly twelve hours earlier. Their trail was cold and washed-out, but careful sleuthing would disclose the direction of their flight. Wiley and John Borders had left only an hour or two earlier, leading a band of men and boys southward across Walker's Mountain to the New River. Harman surmised that this was the wrong direction. The Indians had come out of the Sandy Valley and he believed most of them were from northern tribes. They had been badly mauled in their encounter with the white hunters, had exacted a measure of vengeance, and, in Harman's opinion, would probably return to the Ohio hills, recruit new men, and come back for bolder raids in the winter. The Cherokee whom he knew as Captain John was a formidable adversary, but backwoods gossip among Indians who sometimes traded with the settlers had it that he now had few adherents. The cries and trappings of most of the men Harman had encountered in the forest were Shawnees, and he believed that a painstaking search would disclose that they were now headed toward their towns on the same Guyandotte war trail they had followed on their raid.

He urged the men to eat heartily, get into dry clothing, sleep a couple of hours, and then assemble at the Wiley cabin. He did not need to remind them to see to their rifles, refill their powder horns and shot pouches, and prepare to stay on the trail without rest until the woman was recovered or every hope exhausted. Chastened and humiliated, George Draper offered to accompany them, pledging to stand firm if another fight ensued. But Harman was in no mood to forgive the coward and dismissed him with a contemptuous grunt.

When he stretched himself on his corn-shuck bed for a few hours sleep, Harman speculated on the probable outcome if the little band with Wiley and Borders managed to stumble upon their quarry. The Indians would outnumber them; and for the sake of his neighbors he hoped they had indeed gone north, and that he rather than the distraught Wiley would intercept the "red varmin."

He was soberly realistic about the prospect of overhauling the Indians. They were burdened with a woman whose pace was slowed by pregnancy and the weight of a child in her arms. Indians could be supremely unpredictable. If they, or one of them, wanted the woman preserved they might treat her with considerable solicitude. On the contrary, if she lagged, or became too sick to walk she might be summarily executed. The warriors who captured Jenny were too woods-wise to be pursued without their knowledge and, if overtaken, their captives would be in dreadful danger.

His worst fear lay in the possibility—or perhaps probability—that their flight would carry them westward across the Tug and Louisa into the hills and hollows of the Cumberlands. Seeking them in that maze of trees and brakes would dwarf any effort at woodcraft he had ever undertaken. He calculated that all hope of overtaking them must rest on a strategy of cutting swiftly through the wilderness to the most likely fording places. The Indians could wipe out their trails by wading in streams and doubling back through thickets and cane fields. An attempt to track them would disintegrate into a "wild goose chase," and neither Harman nor his wily riflemen would fall into any such trap. If investigation confirmed his opinion, he would strike off along the Shawnee war trail that crossed the headwaters of the Bluestone and wound south across the Flat Tops, the finest deer run in the southern Appalachians. Then, as rapidly as horseflesh would carry them, he and his men would follow the same broad Indian highway in a westward arc to the best natural ford on the Tug, a place where the water generally ran wide and shallow. There, if his deductions were sound, these savage warriors might be brought to the justice of rifle ball and scalping knife.

The sun had climbed far toward is noonday zenith when Harman and his riflemen assembled at the Wiley cabin, armed and equipped for a long foray into the wilderness. The first to arrive was the indefatigable Henry Skaggs, wrinkled and bearded but almost as slender and erect as one of the youths. While he waited for the others to arrive he leaned on his long rifle and reflected on the many years that had elapsed since he had last seen the fields and villages of his native Germany. Born a European, his boyhood had been spent amid ruins bequeathed by decades of warfare. Now an old man in the American backwoods, he was as thoroughly acclimated to the New World as any man from the Old could ever become. His trousers and jacket were made of soft deerskin fringed on sleeve and leg, and his crudely chopped graying hair was hidden by a comical-looking cap fashioned from a beaver skin. The jaunty coonskin cap with its dangling tail had not yet made its appearance, but the borderers were experimenting and many were abandoning the broad-brimmed felt hats that had long characterized the frontier.

Refreshed by a few hours of sleep and mounted on fresh horses, the men would attempt the double task of vengeance and rescue. Each of them despised the red savages for their raiding, their furtive methods of warfare, their bestial tortures of prisoners and, by no means least, for their race. Unlike the black man, the red man served virtually no useful purpose in the thinking of the borderer. The Negro slave toiled for his master in times of tranquillity and fought for him when the frontier was ablaze with war. But the Indian roamed the wilderness, hunting, idling, marauding. Borderers did not hesitate to take Indian wives and beget swarms of children by them. But these unions did little to erode the general hatred toward the impudent tribes who arrogantly laid claim to a continent and sought to bar wonderful new lands to self-styled "civilized white men." The whites could never truly conquer or fully enjoy the gigantic hinterland until the red scourge was lifted, and the border people were destined to eradicate it.

A search confirmed that the heavy rains had washed out all trace of footprints around the cabin, but the woodsmen did not look for tracks at the shattered door. They surmised that the wily savages had scattered in several directions, breaking up into small bands to come together again at a prearranged destination. Traces of their route must be sought in the hills overlooking the valley.

The ten men in Harman's party dispersed in a similar manner, their eyes glued to the earth, alert for indications of human footfalls. Harman and John and Henry Skaggs went onto the hill to the north and followed the ridgeline for several hundred yards. Then they retraced their steps and whistled to call their companions. The veteran trackers had found convincing proof that the Indians had headed toward the Ohio—proof skillfully furnished by Jenny Wiley.

A pliable deerskin moccasin could be planted on forest loam with scarcely an imprint, but Jenny wore hard-heeled, ankle-length pumps. The heels were more than an inch high, nearly two inches square and capped with cowhide. Several of her heel prints were found along the ridge top at intervals of forty or fifty yards.

The risk she incurred in planting this signal was enough to make the men shudder. In the darkness, her actions must have been difficult to detect, but the savages were alert and suspicious and such actions were unlikely to have gone long unobserved. Four miles from the cabin they passed the last of the heel marks. However, a mile or so farther along, a tiny piece of spicewood lay on the trail where it passed between two boulders. Three more of the fragments were discovered within the next hour, after which no other trace of the red men and their white prisoners was seen. The forest swallowed them completely, as black clouds at midnight engulf a quarter moon.

The party halted and rested. Pipes were smoked and a few handfuls of parched corn were eaten. Up to that point, they had led their horses so they could study the ground for tracks, but now the trail had yielded all the evidence it was likely to divulge. All accepted Harman's opinion that any possibility of success hinged on an astute guess as to their destination and the mountain gaps and river fords they would traverse in reaching it. Then, if the men on horseback—and now hours behind their quarry—could move rapidly enough, they might intercept the savages.

Harman and his companions concluded that the savages had left the Great Guyandotte War Trail in an effort to baffle pursuers. They were, it was supposed, cutting across the country along the network of faint by-trails that laced the wilderness. In the absence of arguable evidence to the contrary, they accepted, also, the estimate of Harman and

Henry Skaggs that eventually the redskins would traverse the Tug at John's Crossing.

John Graham was a North Carolinian who had wandered and hunted in the western mountains for decades. Sometimes he and other hunters brought pack mules into the wilderness, returning with hundreds of pounds of furs and skins. One of the places where the laden animals sloshed across the Tug was known to long hunters as "John's Ford" or "John's Crossing." This same ford was an important point on the westward prong of the Guyandotte War Trail.

There was a long valley which Graham had entered many times, striking its headwaters and following the creek down to its confluence with the Louisa. On some of his expeditions Graham had camped at the mouth of the creek, laying in huge stocks of beaver, bear, buffalo, fox and mink pelts. There the valley was wide and the ground was rich, and there Tice Harman intended to build a blockhouse and make a settlement. All his companions in the present venture and several of the others had agreed to join the undertaking. At the mouth of "John's Creek," they would stand a hundred miles farther within Appalachia than any other settlers had managed to remain. Flowing in from the south to the north the valley afforded an escape route if Indian attacks became overwhelming. Now as they sought Jenny Wiley they contemplated the westward trek they would make in the spring with their wives and children, their livestock and dogs and household "plunder."

These backwoodsmen knew the land almost as well as the Indians they pursued, and they headed for John's Crossing by the most direct course the horses could follow. Whereas the Shawnee trail along the Guyandotte ridge curved in an arc to the north and then westward, there were a number of lesser paths that ran between points on the inside of the arc, and by following some of these "nigh cuts" the total distance to the Tug crossing could be much reduced.

Pushing hard to cross the rough steep ridge known as the Rich Mountain, they struck the Shawnee Path at Rocky Gap. When darkness overtook them, none thought of sleep or rest. When it was too dark to ride, they dismounted and led the horses unrelentingly to the headwaters of the Bluestone. When at last they ate some parched corn and jerky, fed their horses, and rolled in their blankets, the eerie stillness of midnight lay over the forest but they had ascended the Great Guyandotte Ridge. They had traveled far and, if their calculations were sound, had substantially narrowed the gap between themselves and their foes.

Through all the following day, they rushed headlong, sometimes on the ancient intertribal highway, occasionally on intersecting bypaths, but always as rapidly as their horses could carry them. For intervals, they rested the tiring animals by leading them, but afoot or in the saddle they moved without halting in an inexorable race against time.

At dusk on the second day, the men ate well. One of them shot a wild pig rooting in the fallen mast of a hickory, and its fatty flesh made a feast. Chunks of the pungent, almost bitter meat were barbecued over a crackling fire and eaten with the indispensable parched corn. Then, after a quarter-hour of rest sprawled on the leafy mold, they hit the trail again. This night the moon disappeared early behind scudding clouds. The uncertain trail vanished and the men led their horses around precipices, feeling their way down dark hollows and around countless fallen trees.

They retired earlier than on the previous night, however, and because the night was colder, they built a fire. But they were up earlier and because of their ample meal the night before ate only some kernels of parched corn and a few chestnuts. They could no longer afford the luxury of cooked meat.

By nightfall they would reach the Tug River ford and if their calculations were correct they would arrive ahead of the Indians. Then if their luck held and if the Indians were careless, a well-laid ambush would follow. The discouraging possibilities that they had chosen the wrong ford or that the Indians had slipped over ahead of them, reducing to the merest shadow any hope they might entertain of finding them.

In the afternoon, they fed and rested the horses and ate some of the nutritious chestnuts. They reloaded their rifles with charge of fresh powder, pricked the touchholes and primed the pans. They were approaching the Tug River and had found no trace of the savages since the fragment of spicewood more than twenty-four hours earlier. However, about four o'clock Daniel Harman whistled and pointed to the ground. The others took in its meaning at a glance. An Indian lookout had waited under a beech, leaving only moments before. There was one clearly outlined moccasin print in black mold turned up by rooting wild pigs, and as they watched, the stem of a leaf pressed into the soil by the foot sprang up again. Now all hope of surprise was gone and victory could hinge on boldness and fleetness alone.

As the afternoon shadows deepened on the somber hills, the weather became threatening. Black thunderheads built up in the west and unseasonal lightning flickered incessantly. Thunder rumbled with increasingly frequency. The uneasy men feared that the impending storm would be a "roofshaker," washing out trails and turning creeks into roaring floods.

Presently they left the hillcrest and entered a grim and melancholy hollow. Dark and gloomy shadows enveloped the valley and immense trees reared their crest nearly to the ridge tops. They followed a twisting trail worn by the delicate feet of deer, and had to lead their horses down the narrow defile. John Skaggs was in the lead and as he passed under a towering beech he emitted a low poignant whistle. A moment later the men gathered about him and by a flicker of lightning stared in dismay at the woolen-wrapped body of a year-old child. Its white face was flattened and bloodstained, the scalp gone from the crushed skull. Rain commenced falling, spattering into the little pools of blood by the body. A man was left to scoop out a grave while the others, fired with new passions, rushed down the valley toward the ford at its mouth. Suddenly a blinding storm fell upon them, soaking their firearms and their leather clothing.

While the storm raged, they remounted and rode out of the forest to the edge of a narrow canebrake. Pushing through it they looked at the river and for a moment their hearts leaped with hope.

The river, in heavy flow, was swollen far out of its banks. The murmur of the wind and the lapping of the waves on the gray tide cast a dismal spell over the dark landscape.

The chilled and disconsolate horses stood with their heads down in the cold rain while their riders assessed the situation.

A strong swimmer could cross the tide, of that they were sure. He would run a grave risk of drowning, of course, and would probably be carried far downstream, but with a little luck he could make it. But for Jenny Wiley—heavy with child and worn by three hard days on the trail—such a feat appeared unthinkable. Her body had not been found, so it was unlikely that she had met the same fate as that visited upon her child. They had come to the right ford, a marvelous achievement in itself. The savages had probably turned upstream in quest of another crossing place, and if pursued rapidly might be overtaken within moments. Suddenly, however, their speculations were resolved. An enormous spangle of fire leaped across the sky as the storm launched its last bolt and for a second or two the whole valley was brilliantly lighted—the steep hills, the huge trees, the wind-lashed cane and the rushing water. And there on the west bank, under a spreading sycamore on a little flat, lay the Indians, soaked and limp with exhaustion. A few yards closer to the river and half-hidden by clumps of grass lay the skirted and bodiced form of a young woman.

Only the river separated them from Jenny Wiley, but half a continent would not have shut them off from her more completely. Their horses could not swim the stream. They had been ridden too long and too hard and trembled with weariness, wet and cold. None of the men believed he could cross unaided, though the sight of the savages enraged all of them almost to madness. Even if a crossing were to be effected now, the spent men would be in no condition for a fight, virtually assuring that the savages would butcher their captive and scatter in many directions. At dawn, after rest and a good feeding of corn, the horses could carry them over, but until then there was no other course than to find a shelter, cook some food, dry out their garments and rifles, feed and groom their horses and rest for new exertions on the morrow.

At daylight next morning a crossing was effected. The stream was fed by new rains and was little diminished when the reluctant horses moved into the tossing current. The tide seized them and bore them downstream more than a hundred yards before they could find a footing. That the savages had crossed was amazing; that they had carried the spent woman with them was incredible. But on the frontier the unthinkable was often accomplished, sometimes to the borderer's edification, sometimes to his abiding chagrin.

The swim winded the horses again and they rested nearly an hour while the men searched for some trace of the Indians. But the red men had taken no chances. Their trail was not to be found. Strenuous efforts to track them were unavailing. Baffled and infuriated, their pursuers headed across the hills to the Louisa fifteen miles away, reaching it late in the day. No trace of the savages was discovered on its bank. For two days the band wandered about in the land between the rivers, looking for the elusive aborigines and their prisoner. When the waters of the Louisa ran down somewhat, they crossed to its western shore, and for two days sought without success for signs of their quarry. Then, after a day of rest and a meal or two of venison, they began the dispirited return to the settlement. The task of telling Tom Wiley that the Indians had eluded them, slipping almost like water between their outstretched fingers, was one they did not relish. To have come so close and to have failed by so narrow a margin added rankling bitterness to their failure.

But in going, they resolved to come back again to the labyrinth that had swallowed their friend and neighbor, and if fortune smiled a little, they would make it their land.

By then Jenny would long since have crossed the immense Ohio to the hills beyond. From there she might in time be ransomed. Eventually, perhaps, a major expedition of border militiamen would crush the savages and such prisoners would be set free. Until then patience and prayer were the only recourse of those who mourned loved ones captive in Shawnee lodges. Though a few prisoners had escaped, passing like ghosts through the forests and over the great river to their homes, most who tried were recaptured and paid in fire for their daring. Tom Wiley's woman had little prospect for ever coming home again by this means.

CHAPTER ELEVEN

As they moved northward the hills lessened and on the ninth day of her captivity Jenny followed her captors down a low ridge to a rocky promontory. From the ledge of weathered sandstone she looked out upon a broad valley through which flowed a gargantuan river.

The spectacle delighted the young braves. They slapped one another on the shoulders, pointing and saying over and over, "O-hi-o, O-hi-o." Jenny, whose life had been spent in the fastnesses of the Appalachians, gazed in astonishment at the immensity.

The river was far out of its banks. Its floodplain was filled with a vast tawny serpent water. Where the Great Sandy rushed into it, the lesser stream was swallowed up with scarcely a ripple, though it, too, was in full flood. Enormous amounts of driftwood moved slowly past on the sluggish tide. They followed the ridge to the water's edge and stood for a long interval reflecting on the gigantic barrier to their progress. The Indians had cached a number of canoes in a thicket on the southern bank, but the hiding place now lay under many yards of boiling water and the boats had long since been swept away. The disconcerted savages could think of no way to cross the formidable current.

After a time they turned westward, following the hills overlooking the valley. That night for the first time they slept in the open without the shelter of a cliff.

The next day they resumed their westward trek, diminutive specks on the edge of a boiling liquid plain. In the afternoon they found their way barred by another stream flowing from the south into the Ohio—a river settlers would call the Little Sandy. By its banks a prolonged conference was held. A fire was lighted and the warriors sat around it for an hour. A pipe was passed from hand to hand and each of the raiders drew on the fragrant blend of tobacco and willow bark. When the ceremonial smoking was ended, Dull Knife and the other Cherokees, the two Wyandotts and the two Delawares bound their packs and rifles high on their shoulders and plunged into the lesser stream. Within a few moments they stood on the opposite shore and, without a backwards glance, disappeared into the forest.

Black Wolf led the remaining savages and their prisoner up the Little Sandy to the south. They followed the hills above the river, and as their march continued, the valley narrowed. The stream was fed by a startling number of tributaries, all of which they were compelled to ford. They spent the night under a rockhouse and, following the custom to which Jenny had grown accustomed, departed before daybreak, still to the southward.

On that day they turned to the southeast, following a tributary to its headwaters. They crossed through a windswept gap in the mountains into a long and sinuous valley. They followed a narrow but well-defined trail tramped out by the passing of many moccasined feet. The significance of the deep and ancient trace would not be lost on white settlers who would call the pass by the name it still bears, Cherokee Gap.

As the hike continued under immense hemlocks, beeches and poplars the woman fell violently ill. Labor pains assailed her. Her legs and back ached as if struck by sledgehammers. Sharp jabbing seizures laid hold of her and despite her resolution little cries escaped her. No word or look of sympathy came from any of the Indians, but after a time Black Wolf left the trail and clambered up a bank. There they found a huge curving cliff large enough to shelter the company and many others in comfort. Ashes from many old campfires lay in heaps and for sixty feet or more the sandstone ceiling rioted with the same weird black and red figures she had marveled at near the Painted Licks. Under the primitive gallery the Indians laid aside their packs with a finality that marked, for a considerable time at least, the end of their journey, and for Jenny it was not a moment too soon.

At one end of the cliff, an opening led into a lesser cave a half-dozen feet wide and ten feet long. Black Wolf lighted a torch and crawled inside the smaller grotto. After inspecting the chamber carefully, he spread a buffalo hide on the soft sandy floor. He found sticks and leaned them upright across the opening and used another buffalo skin to make an effective screen. Here, he indicated to Jenny, were to be her quarters. Here she would have privacy. Here her child would be born.

The Indians withdrew and she spent the rest of the afternoon in deepening pain. None of the others came about or showed any interest in the woman, but Black Wolf did not desert her. When he was sure she was in travail and that her pains were not merely cramps induced by her long exertion, he treated her with considerable solicitude. He crawled into her stony apartment and felt her forehead in a manner that would have done credit to any physician. He brought her additional coverings against the cold and set a huge torch to burning for both warmth and light. When the carcass of a deer was brought in by hunters he boiled some of the tenderest parts for Jenny and brought her both the flesh and the gruel in which it was cooked.

The birth of her other children had been relatively easy. She had never known the attendance of a physician but had been assisted by experienced midwives, "granny women" as they were called by the Scotch-Irish. And in those births she had had sympathy, a warm dry cabin, and the consolation that her husband was nearby. Now she knew none of these comforts. But notwithstanding the harsh surroundings, this delivery was, in some respects, easier than the others.

Black Wolf went into the forest and brought back a collection of roots, bark and shriveled berries. From them he brewed another black, bitter and extremely pungent decoction which Jenny managed to swallow only with the utmost difficulty. The hot liquid stained her tongue and lips and drew her mouth into a harsh, involuntary pucker, but within moments the medication began to work. She relaxed, the pains came less often and less sharply. She fell into a warm and gentle reverie that lasted for several hours. Near midnight she gave birth to a son. By the flickering rays of the pine torch she saw that he strongly resembled her murdered brother. Even in the twisted little face of the newborn she recognized the chin, the eyes, the determined mouth that had followed the Sellards line for many generations. With a knife BlackWolf had left for her, she cut the umbilical cord and knotted it tightly, then dried his little body with the tattered remnants of her dress. She placed him beneath the warm folds of her buffalo robe and after a few sharp cries the tiny human slept.

When the afterbirth was expelled, Jenny used a sliver of rock to dig a hole and bury it deep in the sandy floor. Exhausted but uplifted by a primordial and immense sense of achievement, she slept, and her last waking thought consoled her that with the vicious Cherokee gone from the party she could expect that Black Wolf and the others would look with favor upon her little son. And in the exaltation brought by his birth there came a renewed determination to escape, a resolution that this child would not grow up as a savage skulking through the forest but would be a white man's son in a proper house and schooled in the white man's ways.

And while she slept the old Shawnee pulled away the hide covering and looked long and intently at her and the baby. No flicker of satisfaction or distaste crossed his features as he dropped the skin back into place and vanished.

For two weeks she was weak and ill. Her strength returned very slowly, and for several days neither she nor Black Wolf was optimistic about the prospects of her recovery. Fortunately, she had a good flow of milk and the baby was adequately nourished from the beginning. But her back and legs were weak and when she struggled to her feet she walked with much difficulty. The many falls she had suffered on the long marches had left her body covered with deep discolored bruises. Her whole abdomen was agonizingly painful for many days. For long periods she lay in a semi-trance, enervated and uncaring, a low and far-off humming in her ears. Sometimes as the baby sucked her nipples she knew the cold presence of death by her side, and only the certainty that her death would assure extinction for the last of her blood drew a resurgence of will back into jaded flesh.

During this period of dependency, Black Wolf did not desert her. He boiled and brought to her bed the best portions of the meat from the campfire. He gathered walnuts and cracked them and gave the kernels to her. He brought the wild fruit of the persimmon tree for her benefit and fetched water in his iron kettle. He fermented crushed corn in clear, cool, sparkling water from the creek and let her drink the weak beer that resulted. He fished in the stream, spearing the black trout with a short iron barb. He baked the fishes in the hot ashes of the campfire and gave her the tender fillets. But though he did these things for her, he did them with the detachment of a veterinarian. Not once did he inquire of her feelings or comment on her condition. His aids—and without them she would have died—were rendered without any trace of emotional commitment.

When her health began to mend, the Indians forced her to resume her labors on their behalf. And there was much to do. They remained at the camp throughout the winter, and rare was the moment in that five-month interval when Jenny was without work to do. The hunters returned daily with the carcasses of deer and the skins had to be scraped, stretched, and tanned for clothing. When she was not gathering wood or cooking, she made garments for herself and the child. The clothing she had worn into captivity was as impractical as it was tattered. To survive and to assure comfort for herself she was compelled to adopt Indian-style apparel.

Black Wolf provided her with a steel needle and an awl. The Shawnee's pack also produced thimbles and scissors acquired by trade or plunder. With these and a keen knife lent her by one of the braves, she produced a coarse thread of thin strips of deerskin. The year had been a good one and the mast was heavy, so that the carcasses were sleek and fat and the skins were soft and pliable. From the hides of the bucks, she fashioned a jacket and skirt for herself. The skirt, which fell halfway below her knees, allowed her much more freedom of movement than she had previously known. Her jacket came down to her hips and was tightened about the waist with a drawstring. Both garments were fringed with strips of leather to carry away water.

When the first such garments were completed she made similar clothing for her son, then an additional wardrobe for herself. Because of the heavy demands made by her captors on her time and strength, to fashion the simple wardrobe required more than a month of sustained labor.

Jenny wondered much about the aborigines with whom her days were passed. Neither Black Wolf nor any of the younger men appeared anxious to leave the isolated camp. They had been away from their villages and women for many weeks, but they showed no restlessness nor any eagerness to cross the river and return to their families. Snow covered the earth for long intervals and they ate, slept, and hunted, or sat about the campfire smoking their pipes and gazing silently into the flames in an unhurrying and timeless sequence.

Though she was a handsome young woman on whose flesh returning health was setting a new glow, none of the warriors appeared to take note of the fact. Tribal taboos would protect her, she believed, until they reached a major village. Then, unless she were sent north for ransom, she would be compelled to undergo purification rites and tribal adoption. In the latter event, she would be handed over to some warrior to bear dusky children and toil in his lodge and cornfields. Still, she could feel no assurance on the matter. Taboos and customs could prove to be frail shields indeed under some circumstances. Above all she feared the effect of alcohol. If raiders were to bring in firewater from a cabin or flatboat, her peril would be immensely magnified. No white captive could be safe once whiskey or rum unleashed the devil spirit that lurked beneath each deerskin jacket.

So she watched always for an opportunity to escape. After the birth of her child she strove to appear contented in order to allay their suspicions. However, she was always alert for a time when all would be away from the camp and the possibility of slipping away would present itself. But no such opportunity came. Black Wolf or one of the others was always near, and though they treated her with acceptance and general indifference, she knew their watchfulness did not relax, and that if she fled they would pursue her promptly and ruthlessly. She kept track of time by marking off the days with a fire-blackened stick on the wall of the little cavern in which she slept. As the days slipped past, her crude calendar told her that her child was nearly three months old and that they had come to the middle of January in a new year.

Jenny had heard the legend of Robert Bruce from her husband. Tom Wiley had related the tale of the king and the spider web and Jenny had felt a deep pity for the hardpressed monarch. She reflected that if they were ever reunited her husband would be pleased that she had named his little son after the gallant warrior-king.

One day as she sat in her little sandstone antechamber

holding the child and crooning a soft lullaby to him, she was startled by a shout from the forest on the other side of the narrow valley. The cry was followed by others and was quickly answered by the Indians lolling about the campfire. One of the voices struck terror in her heart. It was Dull Knife's. The Indians who had crossed the Little Sandy came trooping in accompanied by six or eight others. There was much banter and gaiety about the campfire and the mirth was heightened immensely when Dull Knife unrolled his pack and produced two gruesome trophies—white scalps with long yellow hair. His companions displayed similar mementos of victory, some obviously from the heads of children. Within an hour of their arrival pigments had been mixed and the story of their exploits had been added to the pictures on the rocky ceiling.

Dull Knife paid no heed to Jenny other than to stare with hard, smoldering eyes at her and the child for a thoughtful moment. She learned from their accounts that the newcomers had seen a flatboat floating down the Ohio and had followed it for a long time, hoping it would tie up to shore. Their patience was rewarded. The boat pulled into the mouth of a small stream and two men entered the forest in search for fresh meat. The massacre was quick and bloody. Eleven men, women and children were shot or tomahawked. The warriors were laden with extra rifles, kettles, scissors, spoons, pieces of cloth, mirrors, thimbles and crockery.

Unfortunately for Jenny, they were hungry and there was not much food about the camp. Two young Shawnees were sent out to look for game. They went down the stream and within two hours were back with news that they had found a buffalo bull hiding in a canebrake and had killed him.

Jenny was sent out with stern instructions to accompany the hunters to the carcass and to prepare it for a banquet. Black Wolf went with her to show her what to do.

They found the immense animal lying on its side, one of his hind legs stuck out in a last desperate kick. His throat had been cut and the blood had stained the ground in a wide circle. Jenny had laid her baby in the cane a few yards away and at Black Wolf's bidding began to gut and skin the carcass.

The knife was heavy and sharp, but the hide was thick and tough and she had no help. This was a squaw's work and when a squaw was present no warrior would lift his hand to such tasks. Jenny toiled all afternoon. She managed to split open the creature and drag out the bloated intestines, the stomach and other organs. With a hatchet she cut the carcass in two along the backbone, striving prodigiously to remove the skin undamaged. At sunset the carcass had been cut into quarters. She split the massive skull and dug out the brains. The tongue, too, was saved and prized as a great delicacy.

Black Wolf then directed her to dig a pit in the earth. This she did with her bare hands and with pieces of bark and stone. When an excavation four feet across and three feet deep had been achieved, Black Wolf commanded that she line it with the huge hide, with the hairy side turned down. Thus an effective basin was created. Next she gathered firewood from the surrounding hills—fallen branches, pieces of bark, the dry trunks of saplings uprooted in windstorms. When an immense heap of fuel had been gathered, the medicine man sent a brave back to the cave to bring the others. Jenny was then required to bring water in a kettle from the stream to the hide-lined basin. When it was about two-thirds full she hacked the meat into chunks and dropped them into the pit. A fire was started and round rocks the size of cannonballs were dragged from the creek and dropped into the flames. When they were red-hot she dragged them out with poles and rolled them into the meat-filled pit. They fell amid much hissing and steam and the water quickly came to a boil. For hours the weary woman maintained the fire, heating, retrieving and reheating the heavy rocks until her back, legs and arms ached with an indescribable weariness and her head swam with dizziness and pain. As the water was dissipated by the heat she made fresh excursions to the creek, and as the savages dragged out the hunks of the boiled beef she threw more into the bubbling cauldron.

As the feast progressed, she received the only compliment paid by an Indian during her captivity. Black Wolf, always a light eater, squatted by the fire with a small piece of meat speared on the end of a long knife. After tasting it appreciatively he murmured, "White squaw is good cook."

Until long after midnight she worked at the grisly task. Nor was she allowed to eat any of meat until all the others had eaten their fill and had begun one by one to drag themselves off toward the cliff. She was bone-weary and stained with blood from head to toe. She was soaked with sweat and stank of the campfire and the cooking flesh. Heat from the fire had blistered her cheeks and hands. She could not think of sleep until she had scrubbed her face, limbs and body in water from the icy stream and had put on fresh garments. Even when she and Tige and her baby found refuge at last in the privacy of her grotto she could not relax. A nervous reaction overwhelmed her, her muscles drew up in hard spasmodic knots and she gasped with fatigue, frustration and despair.

When she awoke it was two hours past sunrise. She suckled the baby, holding the hungry little body close to her bosom while the tiny fingers pulled at her flesh. She kissed his nose and forehead, marveling that despite his premature birth Robert Bruce had grown so rapidly that now he was of normal weight for his age.

She emerged from the cave to find the Indians sitting around in groups. From the hostility in their eyes she knew at once that their conversation concerned her. The talk around the smoky fire died instantly and all turned to look at her. Black Wolf's inscrutable mask gave no token of the new ordeal they had planned, but her heart sank like lead with icy misgiving.

Black Wolf approached her. In a combination of English and Shawnee he told her that the child was now three moons old and that the time had come to determine whether he could ever become a great Shawnee warrior. The infant would undergo the warrior's test for courage. If he came through it with a stout heart, he would later be adopted into the tribe and would bring honor to his foster people. But if he failed to display the fortitude expected of him by these cruel and bloodstained creatures? She looked from face to face and from one pair of beady, unwavering eyes to another and a suffocating wave of new horror swept over her as she read the grim answer to her unspoken query. Presently the sinister form of Dull Knife loomed up by her side, his implacable eyes glittering above the broad mouth and flattened nose. He reached for the child, and, as on another occasion of equal desperation and hopelessness, Jenny turned and fled. She dodged him, running down the bank and up the stream.

Again her flight was futile. With shouts of derision the savages sprang after her and within thirty seconds she was overtaken and surrounded. She was held fast while Dull Knife's hard, muscular hands twisted her fingers until she screamed, then wrested the screeching infant from her arms.

Surrounded by catcalling warriors the child was carried down to the stream. While the Cherokee held it, other warriors fashioned a crude raft out of pieces of bark and driftwood bound together with leather strings. When it was completed, the child was laid on it. Dull Knife and a Mingo called Red Turtle waded out into the stream and set the raft in the middle of the swirling pool a dozen feet across. They stood back, watching expectantly. Jenny struggled to go to her child but steely fingers held her on all sides. She leaned forward, her lips open in hope and horror. Every eye was riveted to the pink face of the baby. He looked about him with interest and wonder, and Jenny dared to breathe a little. His miniature hands were drawn up under his chin. A minute passed, then another, and no sound came from him. Bit by bit the raft gathered momentum, turning round and round in the swift current. As the speed increased, the little head turned from one side to the other. The chin turned up as the child arched his back and struggled to turn over. The tiny legs began to kick and the pink hands thrashed about indignantly. Then the mouth opened, the eyes closed and the infant emitted a howl of fear and outrage. Jenny looked at Black Wolf, an expression of unutterable pleading in her eyes. The old man shook his head as if in sadness. She turned her eyes back to the child and screamed with anguish. The Cherokee leaped forward. One of his broad hands swooped the infant from the raft. He held the writhing child by the heels and as he climbed out of the knee-deep water snapped the body back over his shoulders. With a quick jerking motion he brought the head crashing down against a round boulder. The scalping knife flashed and as the seared and transfixed woman watched, her vengeance-mad tormentor ripped the scalp from the head of her fifth child.

The savages straggled up the path to the cliff. The benumbed and brokenhearted woman gathered up the bloody form of her baby and carried it into the forest. She found a little flat place where the soil was deep and black. There on her hands and knees and with a sharp sliver of rock as her mattock, she scooped out a grave. She wrapped the bloody form in the new deerskin clothes she had so laboriously fashioned for it, holding it in her arms for a long time. She kissed its limbs and face and mouth. Then she buried the body, mounding the earth above the grave and setting the stone shard in the earth as a marker. Long afterwards, with leaden feet and heart she trudged back to the camp and her captivity.

CHAPTER TWELVE

In the weeks that followed the murder of the last of her children, Jenny struggled alone and in silence to retain a grip on her sanity. Before his birth, the new life fluttering under her heart drove her to preserve her own. For three months afterwards, she strove with equal fortitude to protect and nurture the child. With his destruction it became increasingly difficult for her to rationalize her own survival in the face of the colossal difficulties that confronted her. For days that lengthened into a fortnight she fought a gray and leaden melancholia that descended upon her flesh and mind and spirit like a wet and suffocating blanket of gloom and despair. It was a mood that left her practically without consciousness for long intervals. So bleak and hopeless had her prospects become and so overwhelming were the trials she had borne that for increasing intervals she contemplated self-destruction as the only attainable release. The prayer to which her father had trained her as both refuge and salvation now yielded neither, and wholly without comfort or peace she slipped close to madness. But like a fever that runs its course, her despair, too, began to ebb and the faint flame of hope survived within her.

By their standards the Indians were not inordinately cruel. Their treatment of her was of the same character they and their progenitors had directed toward captives for millennia. They would have treated a female prisoner from a distant tribe with the same callous disregard for her sensibilities. Indeed, their conduct toward their own squaws was generally almost as harsh—they expected them to cook, to tan hides, to sew, to gather firewood, to fetch and carry endlessly. The test of courage to which they subjected her infant was one their tribesmen had imposed on similar captives for many generations. Warring and hunting were their calling, their avocation, their passion. In the pitiless existence to which history had consigned them, there was no place for weaklings. The timorous—even as infants—were unworthy of adoption into tribes of warriors. The crude test that doomed her child achieved, in their eyes, a rough sort of justice. That it broke the heart of the white squaw mattered little, or not at all. They expected her to endure her bereavement with the same fortitude she would have displayed had the child died of accident or disease.

Fortunately for her own survival, the savages made few demands upon her will or strength during this somber interlude. They hunted, cooked venison over the campfire, smoked their pipes, and lolled in their blankets in graven immobility for incredible intervals. Sometimes she dragged in firewood or worked on the endless deerskins, but in the main she was ignored and lurked in her private little chamber or wandered alone in the snow-shrouded forest.

Almost daily, bands of Indians left and entered the camp. Two or three at a time they detached themselves from the group and disappeared. Jenny assumed, when she thought of it at all, that they went northward and managed somehow to cross the Ohio. Other bands came in and joined the raiders camped under the cliff. The departures and arrivals were generally about equal and through the latter part of the winter eighteen or twenty savages were headquartered under the giant overhanging rock.

As awareness and interest slowly revived within her, Jenny marveled much at the lore and wisdom of the old Shawnee. On one occasion five warriors encountered a group of hunters at a flatboat tied up near the mouth of the Little Sandy. They were Germans floating down the Ohio from Pennsylvania to northern Kentucky. They carried racks of loaded rifles on their vessel and, when attacked, swiftly embarked and from behind the gunwales laid down a sharp and withering fire. The warriors improvidently exposed themselves and two young braves were promptly shot to death and another was shot twice in his right shoulder. His companions brought him to the cave in a coma. Jenny looked at his open mouth and parched lips, his glazed eyes and fever-flushed face, and perceived that death was imminent. She recognized the symptoms of gangrene and did not for an instant suppose that the stricken youth could survive.

But Black Wolf did not surrender. He brought from the forest a collection of roots and leaves which neither Jenny nor any of the warriors was permitted to see or to identify. As always, in preparing his medicines he was extremely secretive, zealously guarding the mystery of his remedies. On a rock fifty yards from the camp he pounded the herbs into pulp. He simmered them in his iron kettle, then used the pulpy paste to make a poultice for the festering wounds.

And, strangely, the man did not die. He languished in delirium for two days, in which the old Shawnee twice removed the poultice and replaced it with another. On the fourth day the fever began to recede. A day or two later he tottered to his feet and began walking about. When Jenny mustered the courage to ask the name of the plants from which he derived his marvelous medicines a scowl flashed across Black Wolf's features and he made no answer.

One day Black Wolf chose four young Shawnees to accompany him and disappeared from the camp. In addition to his hatchet, knife and rifle, each of his companions carried a sturdy leather bag. When they returned on the following day the warriors were staggering under immense loads.

Black Wolf ordered Jenny to gather firewood and bring it to an unused area under the overhanging cliff where the ground was hard-packed and barren, and then to dig a pit in the compact soil. The saucer-shaped depression was about a foot deep at its center and three feet wide. She then dug a trench draining away from the pit to a lesser basin a yard away. Black Wolf pounded the bottom of the trench and both pits with a flat stone until the surfaces gleamed smooth and hard.

He then directed the young men to empty their bags in to the larger pit. The hole was filled with fragments of rock which Jenny spread about in layers. As she handled the bits of stone she saw that slender filaments of lead ran through them and across their surfaces. With her fingernails she was able to scratch off flakes of the soft metal.

Black Wolf then found a smooth, wheel-like slab of rock near the creek and three Indians tugged it onto its side and rolled it to the cliff. It was laid across the stone-filled pit, covering it completely. On it Jenny piled the firewood and, for once, warriors helped her drag in additional fuel. Then a fire was started and maintained for several hours. The heat became so great that for a long time it was impossible to approach the inferno and wood had to be hurled onto it from a dozen yards away.

Eventually the slab of stone turned red with heat. Moments later a glistening stream appeared in the trench, moving slowly at first, then faster and in larger volume. A thin trickle sped down the trench into the lower basin and cooled into a flat and shiny disk of lead. The ingot was nearly a foot in diameter and approximately half an inch thick. Black Wolf used an old hatchet to cut the lead into pieces which he distributed to members of the band to be molded into bullets. Jenny noted that the location of this invaluable metal was made known only to Shawnees. She gleaned from remarks overheard about the campfire that Black Wolf had learned the location of the mineral from French traders whom he had accompanied on a smelting expedition. The Frenchman had recovered a mule-load of the lead and carried it to an Indian village north of the great river. In a lifetime of warfare and wandering the Shawnee chief had unraveled many secrets of the wilderness that were unknown to his companions, and, presumably, to their tribes. Behind his steely eyes lay an encyclopedia of woodlore, warcraft, and crude science.

One day in March when the streams were filled with water from melting snow, the Indians abruptly left their camp and moved upstream. After a mile they turned up a tributary fork and followed it for two or three miles, then crossed through a gap in the mountains and went down another valley. Traveling generally toward the southeast, they passed through a high plateau of rolling land studded with splendid oaks and beeches. Descending for many miles along a deep worn game trail they camped by a huge lick which countless buffalo had trampled into a mire and from which the stream derives the name it still bears—Big Mud Lick. At dawn they broke camp, continuing downstream to a wide bottom where the abandoned huts of an old Indian village stood amid cornstalks in ancient clearings. There they turned north, up Little Mud Lick Creek—a stream tumbling daintily over a series of miniature falls, winding through a deepening little canyon slashed into perpendicular sandstone. At the mouth of that stream stood a breathtaking spectacle—a gigantic beech tree encircled by the painted folds of a fifty-foot rattlesnake. Depicted in red, the serpent reared upward around the barkless column to a point far above the earth where its jaws gaped before an egg it was about to swallow.

Sullen sandstone cliffs extended for hundreds of yards to the north and east. The southern extension of the ledge at the juncture of the two creeks was a hundred yards wide and nearly forty high. Thin, straggly timber grew on its flat top and its sheer sides were pitted with wind-carved caverns. This singular mesa dominated the landscape. The larger stream rushed deep and swift at its western base. Much of Big Mud Lick lay in the dark shadows of giant hemlocks— "spruce pines" to Jenny. Near the old clearings loomed one of the mysterious Indian mounds like those she had seen by the Painted Licks many eventful months before.

Black Wolf led the party along an almost invisible path upward from the water's edge to the crest of the sandstone plateau. They followed the ridge top for a hundred yards, then the dim trail dipped downward to the entrance of a huge rockhouse. The shelter overlooked a rock-studded waterhole sixty feet below.

The opening in which they took up their new abode was high and wide and dry, sculpted by nature into spacious and comfortable shelter. It could be approached only from the top and was practically impregnable against attack. Behind the cavern the level tableland gradually widened into a broad upland much frequented by deer and elk.

The sides of the huge chamber were decorated with the paintings and symbols to which Jenny had become accustomed and the smoke of ancient campfires blackened the soaring ceiling. When they entered their new abode the Indians assumed the solemn mien that Jenny had observed months before when they came to the Painted Licks and the ancient mounds.

The medicine man then gestured for all to follow him to a little clearing on top of the sandstone ledge. Traces of old campfires and the hard-packed ground showed that it had been a gathering place for many years. The Shawnee mixed earth and water and rubbed the mud on his hands and forehead. While chanting in a low singsong voice he threw dust into the air and sprinkled it into his hair. He repeated the same monotonous songs four times, facing each time a new direction. The frowning and melancholy escarpment and the gigantic hemlocks at its base exerted a compelling influence—an influence that fell upon the captive in an eerie feeling that there were, or might be, incredibly ancient spirits in this cliff and grove.

With the warm days of spring the Indians set Jenny to work with an iron hoe they brought from a hiding place in the rockhouse. She judged the cornstalks still standing here and there on the fertile creek bottom to be at least two years old. She dug up the wild cane sprouting in the black loam and with seed corn supplied by Black Wolf planted a considerable field of the grain and smaller patches of beans and squash. When they sprouted and burst out of the soft, spongy soil she cultivated the hills, chopping out the native plants which strove to recapture the cleared space. As spring advanced her cornfield prospered. In the hot moist days of summer it tasseled and soon the Indians were supplementing their diet with multicolored ears of roasted corn and kettles of cooked beans.

In April, soon after Jenny planted her corn crop, Dull Knife left the camp, taking with him more than half of the braves. They departed before dawn, filing out one after the other and with never a backward glance or word. Their expedition had been discussed for days. They were off to join the notorious Cherokee raider, Chief Benge, for a summer of marauding and plundering. Benge's name struck terror in frontier cabins for hundreds of miles across the vast Virginia hinterland. The son of a Cherokee squaw and a Scotch trader, he was audacious, cunning, and cruel. Jenny shivered with dread when she thought of lonely cabins shattered and helpless in their clutches, but the disappearance of the sadistic Dull Knife lifted a shadow from the camp.

With only eight or ten Indians about the camp, her tasks were much lighter and for several weeks she was able to live in relative ease. Storms had flattened many trees near the camp so that the task of supplying the voracious cooking fires was less burdensome. Except by Black Wolf she was largely ignored. One day when she returned from her field, he told her that when the leaves began to fall they would go down the valley to the great river, cross to Ohio and spend the winter in the Shawnee village called Chillicothe. "Then," he said with an emphatic gesture, "white squaw become Shawnee and marry a brave warrior. White squaw be happy in Shawnee town!"

That night, despite her determination to be hopeful, a

new wave of despondency swept over her. For the first time in weeks, she wept when she and faithful little Tige lay down to sleep in her corner of the cliff. The dog alone knew her anguish, or cared.

In September, when the first chill of autumn was in the air, Dull Knife and his band returned, bringing many others with them. Their outlandish scalp halloo resounded from a hilltop to the west, and they came filing in, twenty-three of them.

They carried the carcasses of two deer, and within minutes fires were lighted and the meat was cooking over the flames. All told, more than thirty copper-colored faces squatted in a great circle about the fire.

One of the newcomers was a tall figure and obviously a man of much authority. He was about thirty-five, with broad shoulders, slender hips and a superbly athletic frame. As he moved, his muscles rippled beneath his skin. And unlike that of his fellows, his skin was ruddy, though deeply tanned. He had the black hair and arched nose of the Cherokee but his steady eyes were steely gray, and there hovered about his lips an elusive grimace that betokened malignity and cruelty. He wore breeches of deerskin but his shirt and jacket were trade goods. He carried a superb rifle decorated with much silver filigree and, in addition to a scalping knife, a long double-barreled pistol. Jenny did not have to hear the others mention his name to know the half-breed was Benge.

Once when she was dragging wood to the fire, he turned on her a look of mingled scorn and indifference and demanded, "White woman, who are you?" When Jenny told him her identity he laughed as white men do, but it was laughter without mirth. "I know where Tom Wiley's cabin is," he said, "and I doubt that you will ever see it again!"

The Indians brought with them another man whom Jenny was not suffered under any circumstance to approach or address. He was about twenty-two and white. He, too, was tall and straight with broad sinewy shoulders and well-shaped legs and arms. His hair was long and coal-black, his features superbly chiseled and very handsome. His hands were bound behind his back with thongs of buffalo hide. While the Indians crouched about the fire he lay securely trussed in a corner. Neither food nor drink was offered him and a warrior drove her away when Jenny undertook to give him water.

The prisoner had been brutally beaten. There were dark bruises on his cheeks and traces of dried blood about his lips. And though he knew the fate that awaited him was likely to be horrible beyond words, his eyes brimmed with calm courage and alertness. Both Black Wolf and Dull Knife admonished her to leave the captive alone and many tasks were assigned to her so that she had no opportunity to go near him even for a moment.

The Indians arrived at the camp on Little Mud Lick early in the afternoon and until after dusk the hours were occupied in cooking, eating and noisy revelry. Old acquaintances were renewed and one by one and in great detail the marauders told and retold their tales of raids, murders, plunder and, sometimes, of sharp defeats. Cabins had been sacked and burned. Many scalps had been taken, and a score of them were displayed. The bizarre spectacle of the scalps passing from hand to hand quite revolted the woman, accustomed though she was to seeing the grim trophies. Among those displayed were the pates of silver-thatched ancients, of flaxen-haired children, and one that excited immense mirth—the tight shiny skin from the head of a bald man.

Dull Knife brought a new collection of silver—coins, thimbles, spoons—and using stones for hammer and anvil pounded them into the thin roundish disks he loved to collect. His person fairly gleamed with the metal and a long slender deerskin pouch bulged with the hammered plates.

When a full moon hung like a gigantic lantern above the ridges, the braves tired of their conversations. They had been much more talkative than Jenny had ever seen them before, and as night came on tenseness and eagerness showed through the boasting and chatter. An air of expectancy grew on them. The changing mood concerned the prisoner, and suppressed excitement spread like an electric impulse over the camp.

At last a Mingo warrior stood up and gestured to another. They went to the recumbent captive and dragged him close to the fire. Their companions sprang to their feet and stood around the man, some kicking or striking him. The cords about his ankles were cut away and he stood erect, struggling to keep his balance. Presently the band started up the pathway leading to the top of the plateau and they pushed and hauled him with them. They straggled along, their way lighted by pine torches that cast a hellish light over the whole eerie scene.

Jenny was commanded to aid some of the younger warriors in dragging firewood out of the gloomy wilderness. A blaze was started in the center of the open place where the old Shawnee sachem had wailed his chant to the ancient gods.

Red Turtle, the Mingo, hacked the branches from a young white oak and the prisoner was stood against it. His arms were drawn round the tree and pinioned with cords. Sick and faint, Jenny supposed he would be burned quickly to a crisp, but the savages were about to demonstrate that they were much more ingenious than she had supposed at dragging the last whimper of agony out of dying flesh.

For a few moments the youth's fate was delayed. He talked to them calmly and fearlessly. Jenny noted with vast admiration that there was no tremor in his voice. He said his father was a man of considerable wealth who could pay a valuable ransom if his son's life were spared. Dead he would be worth nothing, alive he would be worth an appreciable store of trade goods. He next proposed that he be allowed to fight for his life with knife or tomahawk against any one of his captors—or any combination of two or more of them. His challenge elicited considerable discussion and some of the braves shouted for its acceptance. But by now their excitement had soared to near-hysteria and most of the savages were in no mood to be diverted by the spectacle of a duel or the lure of cheap baubles and shoddy cloth.

A Delaware who carried a British army musket thrust the end of its steel ramrod into the fire. In moments it glowed red-hot. When he withdrew it from the flames warriors fell on the youth and ripped every stitch of clothing from his body so that his white flesh gleamed in the dancing light. Two warriors seized him by the knees and swept him off his feet, holding him tightly in a squatting position. The Delaware crept behind the man and with a fiendish shriek thrust the red-hot end of the ramrod several inches into his rectum. The scream that tore through the battered throat of his victim brought a hush to the forest and seared Jenny's ears and heart with scars that would last as long as she lived. His cries were deep, raucous, strangling outpourings of agony, injury, indignity and outrage, and brought howls of appreciation from his tormentors. This ingenious trick had been learned from whites who sometimes "reamed" in this manner red warriors whom they captured while skulking near the settlements, releasing them to go howling through the woods.

Then while other warriors held the prisoner a one-eyed Cayuga (the missing eye had been gouged out in a battle with a settler on the Cheat River) went to work with a sharp thin knife. He shoved the keen blade under the skin and sheath of muscles overlying the shoulder blades. A rawhide thong was pushed through from one side to the other and this, too, was drawn around the tree and into a knot. The screaming form writhed, twisted and kicked in unspeakable torment. The flames leaped up and sparks ascended in great showers. Jenny looked into the tortured eyes and the man realized that the white squaw was a captive like himself and threatened by the same fate. In that split second a bond of immeasurable sympathy was forged between them—a bond that lived in Jenny's heart nearly half a century.

A young warrior approached the fire and fired his rifle at the young man's face. The gun was loaded with powder and wadding without a ball, and when the fire flashed from the muzzle the powder residue and charred lint went deep into his skin, burning and blackening it. Others did likewise until every part of his body was black.

The youngest man in the band, a lad of sixteen or seventeen, was pushed forward by an older man and amid much railery from his fellows took his first scalp. The knife was not keen and the flustered boy tugged to loosen the black hair and skin from the skull. It came hard from the living flesh, dragging deep moans from clenched and foam-flecked lips. Then the boy cut off the captive's ears and set them and the scalp to dry at the fire.

A Shawnee piled a few pieces of wood and bark between the feet of the squirming form. Low flames leaped up his legs and toward his genitals. In a new frenzy of contortions, leaps and kicks he strove to scatter the coals and relieve himself of his new torment. But the struggle to evade the flames added immensely to the agony of his blood soaked shoulders. When he lifted his feet out of the flames, the weight descended on to his torn ligaments. The choice was between the agony above and the agony below, and whichever he attempted to avoid swelled the other immeasurably. When he could jump about no longer and hung exhausted on the ropes, his mouth open, his eyes glazed, his blackened legs blistered and cracked, Red Turtle approached and with deft hatchet blows whacked off his legs close against his buttocks, flinging the severed legs to feed the flames. This onslaught brought a new surge of life, the head swinging rapidly from side to side while moans and sobs gurgled from the lips. Blood spurted from the stumps but stopped immediately when a torch was applied to sear the severed veins and arteries. The savages, wildly exhilarated, danced before him. Some applied miniature torches to his chin and the openings of his ears, reviling him in English and in their dialects.

Presently Red Turtle came again, this time severing the arms neatly a few inches below the shoulders. Again the spurting blood was shut off by the quick application of fire, but this time there was no outcry, and the man, so handsome and intelligent an hour before, hung from the tree trunk a blackened torso, a grotesque lump surmounted by a gaping, swollen mouth out of which white teeth glittered eerily, like pearls.

Through all these horrors three of the Indians sat

quietly—Black Wolf the Shawnee, Dull Knife the Cherokee, and Benge the half-breed. They watched as boys might watch a cat toy with a mouse. Benge's cruel features wore a slight smile of contempt. The Cherokee savored the spectacle, puffing calmly on a pipe tomahawk. Only the Shawnee remained wholly impassive, his face an emotionless mask. But as for the others, there could be no question of their sentiment. They howled and pranced before the dying trunk, hideously intoxicated with blood lust and hatred. Their excitement grew as the last moment approached.

From the beginning Jenny yearned with every fiber of her being to go to the man's aid, to cut him down, to give him water, to comfort him. But she knew from harsh and unmistakable experience that any such attempt was doomed to quick and certain failure, resulting with almost equal certainty in similar tortures for herself. Every moment she lingered in the vicinity of the orgy increased her peril and at the earliest opportunity she crept away to her quarters at the rockhouse. As she reached the pathway above the cavern, a whole cacophony of shrieks erupted from the torturers. Involuntarily glancing back, she saw in one swift look the last of the horror. The fire had been fed with new fuel, leaping upward toward the dreadful thing suspended on the side of the tree. An Indian slashed the ropes and with a last indescribable hiss it fell into the flames. The wind carried down to her the vile smell of burning flesh.

A black ocean of nausea suddenly choked her and her stomach heaved with a tumbling fire. Her knees were buckled and she collapsed onto the earth, vomiting out of her tortured vitals the agony and anguish of many days. For a long moment she rocked on the brink of oblivion, half eager to embrace any release. But the retching calmed her and the storm was followed by a new and icy steadiness.

As she struggled to regain her feet the woman considered a precipitate and immediate flight from these creatures who had brought such devastation and misery upon her and her kind. But she choked back the impulse. The forest was dry. By the first light of day they would be on her trail and would overtake her within hours. Then the tortures she had beheld would be inflicted upon her own flesh. Trembling with rage, helplessness, futility and loathing, she steeled her nerves for more patient waiting.

But above her the agitated outpourings continued. Their victim had been reduced to ashes, but the inflamed spirits of the savages boiled in a maniacal frenzy. Guns were fired amid whoops and howls. Sometimes Jenny heard the voices of the three chiefs, seeking to calm them. Usually old Black Wolf could work his way with his younger companions and several times in the hour that followed Jenny heard his voice calling for quiet and an end of the emotional binge.

Soon voices and burning brands told her that a party of warriors was coming to the cliff. They entered the shelter at a run and dragged her out of the little niche in which she lay. Two Cherokees hustled her along the path into the clearing. She was not struck or beaten but the indifference that had long marked their treatment of her had been replaced by a searing hostility. The venom they had directed at their recent victim was transferred to the hapless squaw who had slaved for them through so many months.

She stood in the circle of warriors assembled about the fire, now burning brightly on fresh fuel. She looked into the pitiless faces and smoldering eyes and there was nothing in any of them to give her hope. Black Wolf was expressionless but his eyes avoided her.

As she faced them, their jeers and taunts ringing in her ears, she was swept by a sudden sensation of relief. For an hour she would suffer terribly, then when flesh could bear no more, release would come and an end to it all—an end to endless toil, endless anguish, endless heartbreak. In this new attitude she squared her shoulders, stood up at the stake, and with a contemptuous smile hunted the face of the man who had brought her such immeasurable grief. Dull Knife stood a dozen feet away, his arms crossed upon his chest, a slight smirk upon his thick lips. For a moment their eyes crossed and the true worth of the woman shone in her dark orbs.

Young braves dragged a heap of wood toward her feet and others approached with thongs of rawhide. She wondered with remarkable unconcern on the motives of the medicine man who had shielded and sustained her on so many occasions and now calmly consented to her destruction. Without him she would have died eleven months ago. She was his captive, his squaw destined for adoption among his people, and without his approval they would not tie her to the stake. But no aid came from him and the Shawnee's calm detachment demonstrated that none could be expected.

Suddenly, as heavy hands tore her leather jacket apart at the seams and tugged at the waistband of her skirt, a harsh voice rang out. Every head turned toward him as Dull Knife stepped forward, both hands uplifted. Frozen by the authority in his voice the warriors turned to face him. A silence broken only by the crackling fire fell over the clearing. He looked sternly and intently from face to face. Then speaking in measured tones he astounded the incredulous woman. "This squaw," he said, "is too brave to die. Too strong." He had watched her for nearly a year, he declared. She had done more work than any Indian woman he had ever known. She had borne a child and seen all her children die and had been calm and steadfast through it all. This squaw would be a worthy member of any tribe, and he, Dull Knife, would save her for the Cherokee nation. She was the property of Black Wolf and the Shawnee had agreed that she be burned. But Dull Knife would buy her. He would pay Black Wolf and other members of the band a high price in the white metal that drives white men crazy. He would be proud to take her to his town on the Little Tennessee.

A sharp cry of protest raced around the circle of squatting forms, but Dull Knife was in no mood to tolerate resistance. He loosened a tomahawk in his belt and challenged any man to defy him. The woman, he declared with finality, would not die.

Black Wolf came forward and the two squatted before the fire. Dull Knife sent a young Cherokee to the cave and he returned bearing bags in which the marauder stored his plunder treasures. On the hard-packed ground they haggled over her price. And she came high because all the warriors who had been present on the Walker's Creek raid claimed at least a token share in the woman. Each insisted that he, too, be paid because his participation in the attack had helped bring about her capture.

Dull Knife laid out her ransom without complaint. He emptied the pouches of silver. He stripped himself of the baubles about his neck and in his hair. The thin hammered disks grew upward in stacks, and the fascinated woman, still bound to the stinking stake, calculated that several hundred of the plates of shiny metal changed hands. To acquire her the Cherokee paid over the accumulations of a lifetime of pillage. In addition to Black Wolf, six men claimed part of the loot, and to each went a stack of the disks.

The medicine man scooped all the others and a heap of trinkets into his own plunder bag and, without a glance at the woman, trudged off toward the cave.

Like water rushing through sand, the excitement evaporated. The Indians drifted away. A Cherokee loosened her bonds and the impoverished Dull Knife bade her return to the cave. "Now," he said gravely, "you are Cherokee squaw. Soon I go back to Cherokee people and white squaw go too." Then, with a grating edge to his voice: "White squaw die if she run away!"

At the cliff under her blankets she shook with new dread and horror. When Dull Knife prepared to sleep, he remembered the treasure he had expended for her and that night for the first time in many months she lay tightly bound. Her new master would take no chance on losing her.

Anguish and remorse hounded her like a beast of prey gnawing at her heart. Trussed like a pig headed for market, tormented by ropes at her wrists and ankles and tortured by the pain contorted features of the dying captive, she found the balance of the night unspeakably hideous. Over and over she regretted that she had not escaped long ago or died in the attempt. And while the distressed woman wept in her despair the savages snored peacefully around the campfire. Occasionally one would rise, light his pipe and sit for a while puffing contentedly, gazing into the smoking brands. Their last talk before they fell asleep was a pleasurable recounting of their victim's behavior as he perished in the flames.

After midnight a storm broke over the ridge to the east and for an hour the rain beat down in torrents. The water rose rapidly in the stream, roaring and cascading at the foot of the cliff. The rain stopped before dawn and Jenny heard the Shawnees departing. They filed silently out of the camp, and since Jenny lay bound with her face toward the cliff she was unable to see them go. Thus it was that she did not see again the face of the wrinkled sachem who had saved and then betrayed her.

After the Shawnees left the other warriors returned to their repose or sat puffing their pipe tomahawks. During this interlude exhaustion overcame her and Jenny fell into a brief sleep. When she awoke she was immensely refreshed because she dreamed, and the dream brought her much comfort and inspiration.

The dream was a curious, melancholy visitation. Her experiences in it were of a weird, other-worldly quality like sensations encountered under hypnosis or in a drug-induced trance. To the end of her days she doubted that she had really slept at all.

Jenny dreamed—or imagined—that she was in the total blackness of night. There was a great stillness so deep and vast that she could almost hear the silence beating in her ears. It was cold but presently she felt a warm breeze stirring. In the remote distance she saw a small pinpoint of light which drew nearer, until she beheld that it was a bleached buffalo skull filled with burning oil. She perceived that one of the horns of the skull was held by the hand of a white man, and by the flickering flame of the crude lamp she recognized the features of the young prisoner whose ghastly death she had witnessed only hours before. He was naked and stood tall and straight and unblemished. His white teeth gleamed in a pleasant smile. His black locks fell on his forehead and about his cheeks. He beckoned soundlessly and walked away, and his steps were confident and unafraid.

She followed him a great distance. The lamp illuminated her footsteps but dimly. Her guide escorted her past precipices out of which came the roaring of great winds and mighty waters. He led her up rocky escarpments and down faint paths and over the crests of towering peaks. Huge trees overshadowed her way and a great weariness grew upon her and she longed to rest. Once the path they followed forked and by the uplifted light she saw a bird hopping before them. The bird went to the left and the apparition with the lamp followed it along the same trail until if flew away. At last they came to a broad plain and came out upon its brink the young man smiled graciously and pointed across the river. The light from the lamp swelled to the brightness of day and she saw beyond the stream in a broad field a frontier blockhouse, with people and cattle about it. She called to them, and they turned toward her and she saw from their expressions that they had heard and intended to give her aid.

At that moment her dream was interrupted. A rude hand shook her and she opened her eyes to see the face of Dull Knife close above her own. He unbound her, and as she rose to commence a new day in the horror-infested camp, she was a reborn woman.

Jenny lived in a culture that accepted without question a belief in divine intervention, and she had no doubt that the figure in her dream was the spirit of the young man sent by the God of her fathers. She knew then, with a strong conviction, that the hour of escape and deliverance was near.

After they had breakfasted in the usual fashion all the warriors except the Cherokees filled their packs with their belongings. The Mingoes, Cayugas and Delawares made the peace signs to their southern brethren and filed down the valley toward the northeast. The long encampment in the narrow valleys of Kentucky was breaking up. The northern Indians were heading for their villages beyond the river, and Dull Knife's band would soon head southward toward the Little Tennessee.

After the departure of their fellows only fifteen remained within the camp. They talked in low monosyllables for a considerable time, then Benge and four warriors took their leave. They went eastward looking for more scalps, promising to see Dull Knife and his followers in their village before winter. As he passed Jenny, the half-breed spoke to her: "White slut, if ever you get back to your people, tell them these woods are stakes for their burning!"

CHAPTER THIRTEEN

The Cherokees who remained at the camp after the departure of the northern Indians were almost without meat and intended to lay in a supply of smoked venison to sustain them on their long hike to the south. About noon Jenny was bound again, and this time, in addition to the thongs at her hands and feet, she was made fast to a slab of fallen sandstone.

The savages left the rock house and climbed onto the little plateau. Straining her ears, she heard them pass through the ancient council clearing. They would hunt for deer and elk in the high country on the head of Little Mud Lick and would probably return with carcasses long before nightfall. Now at last was the time of her deliverance if by any exertion of muscle and will she could escape from the ropes.

Carefully, methodically, determinedly, she tried the rawhide at her wrists. The thongs were small, not much thicker than shoestrings, and they bit deep into her flesh when she pulled against them. The leather was dry and did not yield. She realized that the knot was secure, the cords tough and strong, and that any hope of breaking or slipping out of them was insignificant.

She struggled with the cords at her ankles with similar results until she lay panting with open lips and heaving bosom. Presently it began to rain again and water dripped from the edge of the cliff. She lay about eight feet from the rim of the overhanging rock and the sandy floor was dry and hard. She knew the tendency of leather to stretch when wet, and the rain offered her a new hope of escape if she could manage to elude the ropes that bound her to the stone.

She began rolling from side to side. The rawhide went round the rock twice and two strands held her to it. Struggling until perspiration ran down her nose and cheeks she felt one of the cords relax. Frantically she renewed the effort and rolled away. With her eyes bulging from exertion she turned over until she lay face down with the water falling freely on her back.

Her friend Tige had remained by her side and he watched all her efforts with fascinated gaze. Once he barked excitedly, wagging his tail in a frenzy of well-wishing. Now as she lay soaked and breathless he ran close to her and licked away the tears of hope and vexation that gathered on her cheeks.

When the cords were thoroughly soaked she tugged at them. They felt slippery and began to yield. Rubbing her wrists against one another until they were chafed and bleeding, she felt the left hand slip slowly through the loosened strands. When her benumbed hands were free, a full five minutes elapsed before she cast off the cords that bound her ankles. Then she stood up, immensely exhilarated by the possibility of regaining her liberty and outwitting her brutal overlords.

She listened intently for footfalls, the creak of wet

leather against brown shoulders, the plop of soaked moccasins on the rocky path. But the only sound was the tumbling water in the creek below, and the spatter of rain drops from the great trees onto the dank mold of the forest floor.

She moved quickly. She searched the packs of the warriors looking for weapons. She wanted a firearm, but there was none at the camp. She armed herself with a well-honed knife and a long-handled steel hatchet. She poured two quarts of parched corn into a leather pouch and slung it across her shoulder, then searched all the packs scattered across the sleeping skins for the scalps of her children. Even in her haste she hoped to avoid having them hang in the smoky rafters of an Indian lodge, but they were not to be found. Fortunately she was wearing new moccasins, and for warmth and a little shelter against the rain she flung a deerskin shawl about her shoulders. Tige followed her eagerly, sensing an adventure, but she dared not allow him to accompany her for fear of yelp would reveal her whereabouts to pursuers. Steeling her courage, she lifted the hatchet to dash out his brains but his tail wagged and his soft brown eyes sparkled with trust. Her resolve evaporated. The hatchet was laid aside, and after an affectionate embrace she bound him tightly with the thongs that had held her—an act of mercy that would place her own life in horrible jeopardy before many hours. As she left the cliff, the dog whined in bewilderment and surprise.

She moved out resolutely, hoping to gain three or four hours before her escape could be discovered. Every precious second would have to be utilized to the utmost, with her cunning and woodcraft pitted against those of the savages for the highest of all stakes. She strode to the clearing, leaving clearly visible footprints here and there. Then, slipping out of her moccasins, she backtracked herself to the top of the cliff shelter. Following a trail down to the edge of Little Mud Lick she put on her moccasins again and stepped into the water. Wading into the middle of the crystalline current she squared her shoulders and started homeward.

The stream bed was strewn with gravel and slabs of stone. The water was cold and babbled and swirled about her feet, damping her elation and bringing a new appreciation of the task on which she had embarked.

She passed the lower falls of Little Mud Lick where it cascaded noisily into the larger stream. A mile from the camp Big Mud Lick flowed into a larger stream known today as Big Paint Lick, and the water rose to her knees. Crossing Big Paint Lick she waded in shallow water on the opposite shore until, a few hundred yards downstream, a creek flowed in from the southeast. This stream was swollen out of its banks and the water jostled her as she gazed up the gloomy valley, where dark hemlocks and pines towered ominously. Rain began falling, softly at first and then in cold and leaden torrents, from the clouds that brushed against the ridge tops and sent wisps trailing downward to the valley floor. For a minute or two she hesitated, uncertain whether to enter this thoroughfare and follow it toward its source or to pursue Big Paint Lick toward the Big Sandy. The latter, she decided, would be the route her pursuers would be most likely to follow. Abruptly she resolved the issue, and, struggling in waistdeep water, set off up the rugged valley.

The twisting, winding watercourse was eight or ten yards across and flowed in the pristine purity it had known from the beginning of time. The somber trees towered skyward like the columns of a titanic temple. By the time she had struggled against its tide for a couple of miles her strength began to flag. It was apparent that she must leave the water, risking tracks discernible to the ubiquitous savages. She looked for a place where she could step onto a smooth stone, and thence to firm ground. She found a little covert where fall flowers grew on the crest of a huge rock. Beyond it was a thicket of mountain laurel. Peering into it in the fading light of the dying day she made out the faint outline of a game trace.

Drawing herself cautiously onto the stone, she sat down and, removing her moccasins, wrung the water out of them. Then, moving barefoot and placing her feet carefully, she climbed gingerly up the bank. Turning sideways to slip between the laurel trunks without breaking or disturbing their branches, she stepped onto the little trail. Slipping again into her moccasins she set out at a rapid pace. She walked Indian-fashion, setting one foot directly in front of the other. Methodically she placed her feet squarely on the ground, minimizing their friction against the soil. She wanted no scuffing of leather against dirt or stone or moss to tell some sharp-eyed tracker of her passing. To economize her strength she made her steps long and bold.

A mile after striking the trail the stream forked. The dim trace divided, with one branch going to the left and through a gap in the mountain toward the southeast—the direction she sought to follow. The other turned toward her right and disappeared in the direction of a lower notch to the southwest. Jenny had no idea where any of these trails led, but she wanted to avoid for a while the much-traveled Indian trails on the Big Sandy. As she pondered the divided path, she saw a heap of deer dung a dozen yards away on the left prong of the trail. While she watched, a bird remarkably like the one she had seen in her dream came down to peck it. Leaving the droppings, he hopped along the trail, and Jenny saw in this the good omen for which she sought. A surge of elation warmed her despite the icy water dripping from her clammy deerskin clothing. She forged ahead to the left and the bird fluttered into the timber and disappeared.

Presently the trail divided again, and again one fork turned sharply to her left, disappearing toward the east. But Jenny did not follow that prong of it. She pursued the gap towering in the mountain above her. Passing through it, she looked down upon a valley about two miles long. She rested under a tree eating a handful of the parched corn and getting her breath again. A hundred yards above her a black opening loomed in the face of a cliff. Mossy rocks partially concealed the entrance. Two glossy black bears emerged from it and stared at her. They were fat and indolent, their hibernation soon to begin. Inquisitive cubs peered from between their parents' legs, staring at her with profound curiosity. Trees growing in the gap were torn and battered by the claw marks of the powerful and short-tempered creatures. She had been told by hunters that they denned, sometimes a dozen or more together, in such caverns on the tops of the windswept hills.

The trail led away from the valley and around a bench on the hillside, but Jenny continued down the slope and presently, as insurance, reentered the creek trickling down from the gap. Darkness—relieved occasionally by a sickly half-moon that sometimes darted form behind the cloud banks—overtook her as she did so. All night the driven woman followed the streams, walking in or near them. Each was a tributary to a larger one and must lead ultimately to the Big Sandy, a fork of which pointed toward Walker's Mountain. After midnight the moon vanished altogether behind a thick pall of fog and clouds. The forest dripped moisture and its voice was muted. All the usual noises of the wilderness night—the hooting of owls, the scurrying of feet, the cry of bobcats, the rustling of wings, the baying of wolves and the barking of foxes—were stilled. Mercifully, the rain ceased to fall, and in almost total darkness, she groped her way, accompanied by no sound except her own footfalls, the murmuring water and the scarcely audible sighing of wind through the tree-tops. Her pace was slow and she traversed only a few miles between dusk and dawn.

In the predawn, when the first faint luminescence tinted the east, she sat down exhausted. She ate some more of the corn and, overcome with cold and weariness, fell asleep. When a brief patter of rain awakened her, daylight had penetrated the mists. She lay on a deep and ancient bed of moss in a grove of huge beeches. The stream flowed gently through an almost level valley, proof that merger with a greater flow was not far distant.

Bending down she drank deeply, catching her reflection in the pale light. Her leather jacket, the straight black hair falling in bound strands on each shoulder and her deep weathered tan were Indian. With a start she realized that her year in the wilderness had converted her almost to one of its own.

Again she drank from the stream, then paused a moment to ponder her situation. She had covered many miles over a devious and, as she believed, unpredictable course. Hopefully, she had left no telltale signs, but there could be no doubt that Dull Knife and his Cherokees were seeking her with immense stealth and cunning. She had an overpowering intuition that white people were near. The spirit with the lamp had disclosed it. The bird had propitiously set her on a path toward a white settlement. That settlers had come into this land, and avoided discovery by the numerous bands of red marauders headquartered at the cliff throughout the summer was most unlikely. Still, she had heard no mention around the campfires of any white intruders in these ancient hunting grounds and, she wistfully supposed, a little fort might have been set down somewhere in one of the valleys without being detected by the wandering red men. On the other hand, the captive might have been abducted from such an outpost, its defenders being too numerous for direct assault even by the more than thirty braves she had once counted.

Rain poured in from the west, this time in earnest, ringing metallically across the top of the forest. The deep coughing cry of a hungry mountain lion reverberated from a ridge top. Birds twittered and fell silent. A little rivulet ran down the hard-packed trail, and Jenny looked about for a shelter in which she might sleep awhile longer, for her brief nap had done little to restore her strength.

A dozen yards away an ancient tulip poplar lay where it had fallen in some titanic struggle with the wind. Decay had hollowed out the interior of the immense column, and, standing at the root end, Jenny stared into a wooden cavern. A tangle of spiderwebs spanned the opening with a maze of fragile filaments in which countless insects had been trapped. She dropped to her knees and started to crawl inside, reaching up with her hands to brush the impediments away. But she thought better of it. Instead she carefully detached them from the bottom of the rotted bole. Lying down, she slid backwards under them. When she was within, she carefully reattached the webs to the rotted wood. As she backed deeper into the trunk, she scattered handfuls of the mold before her to obliterate signs of her passage. Six feet from the entrance she came to a halt, soaked and chilled but beyond reach of the new downpour. Cradling her face in her arms, she whispered a prayer of thanksgiving and hope, and, tired but optimistic, fell asleep to the deep droning of the rain against her shelter.

When she awakened, it was broad daylight and the rain had ended. A sheet of sunlight warmed the moss and ferns beyond the entrance of her shelter. A deep, guttural voice struck with an icy stab into her heart—the petulant tones of Dull Knife. In a fragment of a second she was fully alert, horrified that her best efforts had been futile, that the Cherokee who had slain her family and claimed her by purchase had overtaken her. He stood no more than a yard from her and he and Red Turtle discussed her flight. Jenny scarcely breathed at all. The men leaned against the huge trunk. Through the wooden walls she could hear the crunching of parched corn as their teeth crushed the hard grains. Presently two others joined them, coming from downstream. With exasperation and bewilderment, they expressed their chagrin and amazement at her trackless escape.

With deep vexation, Dull Knife conceded that the woman had eluded them. She had left no mark, passing over the land as elusively as a bird. They had not found so much as a displaced leaf or pebble to indicate her trail. No Indian, no white man Dull Knife had ever known had moved through the forest so tracelessly. He grunted in wrath and a tomahawk bit deep into the rotted wood, accompanied by a vow of vengeance upon her. A silence ensued in which it appeared that the tomahawk had inspired them. Red Turtle raised the possibility that she might be anywhere, even within the very tree against which they leaned. At precisely that moment the black and white face and pointed ears of Tige appeared at the entrance. Wriggling with joy, he looked at her and whined. Jenny closed her eyes and sagged with despair. Overwhelmed by the new enormity that now swept her toward total disaster, her stomach suddenly tightened into a hard, heaving knot and the world spun and danced as in an earthquake.

But her weakness was only momentary. With a deep-drawn breath she regained a measure of composure and her grip tightened on the handle of the keen knife.

Tige's whining turned to a friendly yelp and she heard footfalls as one of the savages approached the dog. Jenny's heart stopped beating and her breath halted in her frozen nostrils. Discovery now was certain. Her only hope was to fight so vigorously when they dragged her out as to bring upon her head a quick and merciful death.

With a muttered imprecation Dull Knife, too, left his place by the log. She heard his soggy moccasins passing over the rain-soaked loam. At that instant a ground squirrel darted from the edge of the log and barking furiously the dog sprang after it. In the morning sun she saw the Cherokee's sturdy, leather-fringed legs and broad feet stop before the opening. For a long moment he stood there, but he did not stoop to look within. Instead, his thick, copper-colored fingers swept across the opening, brushing lightly against the cobwebs that blocked it. Then with a grunt of disappointment, he returned to his place by his companions.

For two or three endless minutes the men rested, then,

calling to the dog to return and follow them, they set off downstream and Jenny heard them no more. An hour later, she cautiously emerged and resumed her flight. A short distance brought her to the end of the stream—Little Paint Creek. The stream into which it flowed was a river, the western prong of the Big Sandy along which a year before she had been led like a tethered brute into captivity. Some of the weird painted trees lined its bank, and as she pondered this rain-swollen barrier, a flight of passenger pigeons numbering scores of thousands settled in the cane-grown bottoms beyond. Squirrels chattered and a peccary snorted and fled. A family of bears looked down at her from a tall chestnut, and the eerie howling of wolves sent a chill down her spine.

Occasionally she left the trail and hid to listen for the sounds of men. From the forest came the near-silence of animals, insects and birds, the rustle of leaves and the ripple of water, but of men she heard nothing.

The valley was wide and green with broad brakes of cane. It was the land above the Painted Licks. The trail soon merged with the one she had followed in the previous autumn, and she recalled some of the landmarks. She was on one of the broad highways that followed the Big Sandy from Virginia to the hills of Ohio, the same trace Harman had followed many times on his hunting expeditions.

After she had followed the river a mile or two, the path ascended a little eminence of land. Coming to its crest, she looked across a field of cane dotted with a few patriarchal poplars. The river swept around a huge bend, enfolding a wide flat bottom. But this expanse was different! The cane had been uprooted and several acres of corn had been planted, and beyond the corn, in a clearing, stood a little blockhouse surrounded by a palisade of sharpened timbers—the same little post she had glimpsed in her "vision"! Women and children stirred about its doorway and a faint wisp of blue smoke escaped the mud-daubed chimney.

As she gazed toward the absurd little bastion—so near and yet so far away—her condition can scarcely be imagined. Twenty-four hours had elapsed since her flight began, three-quarters of which she had passed on the trail. She had spent hours in cold water, sometimes waist-deep and swiftly running. She had endured driving rain and chill winds in stretched, clinging leather clothing. She had eaten nothing in that time except a couple of handfuls of waterlogged parched corn, and had slept once briefly. She had endured terrible tensions of nerve and mind and spirit, fearing each moment that she would encounter a band of shrieking avengers intent upon her destruction. Behind her, like links in a chain, lay a series of mangling traumas, any one of which could have crushed a person of strong will. Now in the aggregate they suddenly fell upon her taut nerves like the edge of a razor on a fiddle string. Her incredible exertions had brought her to the brink of deliverance, but she was still in terrible peril. The swollen river carried almost as much water as when she had first seen it a year ago. Then she swam it, but only with the aid of two sturdy warriors. To attempt a crossing now would end her miseries and crown her achievements in a swift death by drowning. And yet she knew with certainty that unless she crossed quickly she would not cross at all, because the fast-moving and restless Dull Knife would come this way as soon as he realized that she was not to be found downstream. Mustering the last reserves of her strength she ran down the river bank, waving her arms and shouting, "Help! Help! I am Jenny Wiley! Won't somebody help me across the river?"

The little figures beyond turned to look, one man, several women, a group of children. Jenny shielded her eyes against the sun and looked intently. It was old Henry Skaggs whom she had known since girlhood. "Henry Skaggs," she called. "Henry! Henry! Don't you see who it is? It is Jenny Wiley, Tom Wiley's wife."

There was a calling of voices among the people at the little settlement, then the old man ran into the diminutive fort and returned with a rifle, powder horn and shot pouch. When he reached the river, he looked at her reflectively, stroking his long gray beard. She looked across the expanse of swift water and shouted a new plea: "Get me across, Henry! The Indians are nigh and may catch me anytime!"

Apprehensively she looked down the trail for the faded trade shirt of her nemesis, but for the moment at least nothing moved there. She called again and Skaggs recognized her voice. He shouted back, cupping his hands to make himself heard across the tumbling tide, but his words brought her no comfort.

He was the only man at the blockhouse. All the other men had gone down the river and were not expected to return until after nightfall. They had taken the only boats and there was no raft.

CHAPTER FOURTEEN

For several minutes after the people at the settlement had convinced themselves that the squaw-like woman on the far bank was Jenny Wiley, they remained extremely wary. There was much calling back and forth between Skaggs and the women at the blockhouse and the increasingly distraught woman who implored their aid.

At last the old man sternly demanded, "Jenny, be truthful now! Are there Indians with ye? Are they usin' ye fer bait?" Jenny understood their predicament and in a voice vibrant with sincerity shouted back at him, "No, Henry no! The Indians are not here yit, but they are behind me and if ye don't hurry and fetch me across they will catch me fer sure!"

"How many are there, Jenny? How many are atter ye?"

"Only four, Henry," she shouted back, holding aloft four outstretched fingers, "but more are about, and they'll all git here afore long!"

Assured at last that the Indians were not using her as a pawn to draw them into a trap, they came streaming toward the river. The indefatigable Skaggs carried two long rifles and a powder horn and shot pouch. She recognized the plain, hard, pragmatic faces of Mahala Hawes, Martha Draper and

Mary Harman, and there were three or four others whom she did not know. Each of the women carried a rifle, shotgun or axe.

Once embarked upon her rescue, they toiled prodigiously. On the riverbank, a dead mulberry towered starkly against the sky. The weathered branches had fallen and it endured as a tall, white column. Laying his rifle close at hand, Skaggs began chopping at the tough base of the tree. Mahala Hawes sank her axe into the opposite side and the hollow, rhythmic strokes rang out. The dry wood was hard and the axes often bounced away without biting into the tree. To the agitated Jenny an age passed before the tree swayed and crashed to earth. She dreaded the eternity that must pass before the trunk could be chopped into smaller sections to be fashioned into a raft. Fortunately, however, the fall broke the trunk into three pieces. Wading into a spit of shallow water and tugging until their faces were crimson, the women and children dragged them together in the shallow water and held them against the tugging current. Other women cut grapevines, and children hastened to the blockhouse for deerskin ropes. With the pliable vines and the leather thongs, they bound the fragments of wood into a clumsy and thoroughly unstable raft. In the meanwhile Skaggs cut a pole fifteen feet along. Women laid a loaded rifle and a double-barrel "polk-stalk" shotgun at his feet and he pushed the clumsy craft out into the current. Jenny looked anxiously down the trail. Now cold sweat stood on her face, and a smothering sensation swept over her. The Indians might have gone for miles downriver or, on an impulse, some or all of them might have turned upstream again, in which event the shouts and the sounds from the axes would surely hasten their footsteps. They could bear down upon her at any moment, rifles and hatchets in their hands, and bloodcurdling war whoops pulsating on their lips. Her heart beat wildly when the hopeless little raft pushed into the main current, whirled round and round and then rushed furiously downward.

The old backwoodsman's beard flew in the wind. His eyes rolled wildly as he pushed the pole frantically against the sandy river bottom. Struck by driftwood, the raft lurched wildly and appeared to be in danger of breaking up. For a moment, he lost his footing and fell to his knees, but he scrambled up again and with a strength that would have done credit to a youth, continued to struggle with the current. By scarcely perceptible degrees, the rude float crept across the main current with the woman accompanying it on the shore. Even after it had passed into calmer waters on the west bank, the craft was difficult to manage. Twice, it became entangled in dense willow bushes, and when at last it floated to within dozen feet of the shore Jenny waited no longer. Endowed by desperation, with a new strength, she dove into the water and swam to the raft. "Now, Henry," she gasped, "push with all yer might. I'll help push it across the river!"

Again, the aged stalwart toiled with infinite patience and determination. Again, the raft whirled and lurched, the ropes and vines stretching until the timbers stood inches apart. When it reached the middle of the stream the craft presented an incredible spectacle: the old man in buckskin, with wild eyes and flowing beard, his skinny but still sturdy arms churning the water with the pole, and the deeply tanned and leather-clad woman clinging to the end of an absurdly frail and awkward raft and flailing the water with frantic kicks.

Powered by desperation, the strange pair gradually brought the craft across the current, but in doing so they drifted far downstream and when the raft touched shore they were a mile and a quarter below the blockhouse.

As soon as they were on dry land again, they started up the river, without hesitating to rest. Jenny was so delighted to see a white, friendly, welcoming face that she distracted Skaggs by hugging him and kissing him on both cheeks. Wet, weary and breathless as she was, she was in no mood to tolerate delay. With the shotgun in her hands, she sped with long strides toward the fort. But Skaggs could not stand for long the pace she set for him, and they came to a halt under a tree. He leaned against the trunk, sweat glittering on his forehead. For several minutes, he sucked his breath through parted lips, gazing at Jenny all the while—at her browned skin, strong work-roughened hands, fringed leather jacket and skirt. "Jenny," he panted, "ye're almost like a squaw. If I had seen ye in the woods I would have scalped ye fer an Indian."

Three of the women and some boys of twelve or fourteen met them a couple of hundred yards from the fort. The women embraced her amid exclamations of pleasure and astonishment and hurried her toward the gate. But before they could pass within, shouts resounded from beyond the river. Looking back, Jenny saw four savages dart from the cover of the trees. Brandishing rifles and tomahawks, they ran toward the riverbank. In the forefront was a sturdy, thickset figure in buckskin leggings and trade-cloth shirt, with a rifle grasped by the muzzle lying across his shoulder. Eagle feathers protruded from his hair and a tightly drawn scarf encircled his forehead. The pale sunlight glittered against a few bits of silver in his hair. Dull Knife's deep voice reached her, a note of entreaty in the guttural tones, "Jenny, come back! Honor! Honor, Jenny, honor!"

She measured the distance and realized that they were too far away for an effective shot, but Henry Skaggs raised his piece and fired. The bullet fell short, making a little splash on the river. The voice of the Cherokee changed into a deep spine-chilling war cry. He, too, sighted and fired, the ball kicking up a spatter of sand a dozen yards behind Skaggs. Then turning his back to them and emitting a diabolical cry, the Cherokee derisively patted his buttocks and disappeared into the cane. A moment later, the gate slammed shut behind Jenny and three thick wooden beams locked it fast.

The place was kept in readiness for siege all the time, but in the three-quarters of an hour since Jenny had first called to them, the women and children had been busy. Barrels had been filled with water and additional firewood had been carried in. Vegetables drying in the autumn sun had been stored in the loft. Cattle and horses had been brought from the forest and shut up in the pens. The children had rounded up a sow and litter of pigs and fastened them in one of the cabins.

The weary Jenny took up a position at one of the loopholes. She carefully inspected the rifle one of the women had handed her—a lean .35 caliber with an excellent flint. The powder horn was almost full and Skaggs gave her a dozen bullets and a handful of flax lint for patches. Extending the barrel a foot outside the opening, she drew a bead on a walnut forty yards away. She set the rear trigger with a quick jerk, then, sighting carefully, with a tiny pressure on the hair trigger she brought the flint crashing down on the steel frizzen. There was a dull roar and the walnut shattered. Jenny smiled approvingly. She was still a first-rate shot and as long as that rifle remained in her hands, no Indian would drag her into the wilderness again.

No more was seen of the warriors and no sound came from them. Only four had been seen—Dull Knife, Red Turtle and the two braves who had joined them at the fallen tree. But within a few hours, the eight others could be brought in and a band of twelve skulking in the forest could put the garrison in severe straits.

Jenny was called upon to recount her adventures, and she did so, from the gory beginning to the hectic end. She told her story briefly, tightly, without wasting words or sentiment, and her listeners, schooled in frontier hardships, required no retelling. They measured the unspeakable horror of her misfortune and saw in her return vast courage, an almost superhuman hardihood and much good fortune.

The settlement onto which she had stumbled was six months old. Tice Harman had led the colony into the wilderness early in the spring, and they had toiled all summer—eleven men, seven women and twenty-two children—to build the blockhouse and four small cabins and to join them together with a palisade of sharpened poles. A dozen acres were in corn, and the trees in another dozen acres had been deadened for new clearings in the coming spring.

In midsummer, a man named Vancouver and a company of men had come down the Tug Fork in canoes. Thirty miles below Harman's station at the mouth of John's Creek they had built a station at the juncture of the Tug and Louisa Forks. Vancouver was an Indian trader and a land speculator. He hoped to survey an immense boundary, obtain a grant of title from the Virginia government, then import settlers. On the day before Jenny's return, a hunter from Vancouver's station had come by Harman's settlement and reported that Vancouver had put a still into operation and had boiled off a barrel of whiskey. On the morning of Jenny's deliverance, Harman and all the men except Henry Skaggs had gone down the river to visit Vancouver and his men, to swap news with them and to drink some of his liquor. They had been so busy all summer building, planting, hunting and patrolling against Indians that they had had no opportunity to set up this indispensable fixture of the frontier. Harman loved a dram—as, for that matter, did the others. They could not return before nightfall and now they ran a frightful risk of being ambushed. There was little the people inside the blockhouse could do to warn them. A scout going out to seek them would have to follow the riverbank. The Indians could have improvised a boat or raft within an hour or two and might be encountered on either or both sides of the river. Under these circumstances anyone slipping out of the fort would be observed and promptly slain or overwhelmed and captured. With rifles and axes at hand they waited, every nerve strained with watching and listening. At intervals a rifle was fired, and from time to time Martha Draper blew raucous blasts on a ram's-horn trumpet—sounds calculated to put the party on notice that death lurked in the black night around the fort.

CHAPTER FIFTEEN

At dawn of the day of Jenny's return—while the rain-soaked and trail-worn woman was seeking a little rest in the hollow log—the tiny settlement cautiously awakened. Doors were opened and keen eyes swept the mist-shrouded forest. Keen ears listened for suspicious sounds. The dogs were called in and counted. A missing or mangled dog warned of Indians lurking nearby. The borderers were light sleepers and their canine outguards were their shield against the approach of enemies who could move as silently as the wind.

But on this morning all was well. From the awakening forest came the chattering and rustling of countless squirrels, the gobbling of wild turkeys and the raucous cawing of crows. The sounds were assayed and found authentic. Even the most skilled and articulate red woodsmen could not duplicate precisely the calls of forest bird and beast. To the sensitive ear of the borderer the red man's voice added a faint throatiness that betrayed it, even when the cries were accepted as genuine by the forest creatures.

By the first rays of the ascending sun, the cows were milked in their pens. A few handfuls of corn were distributed to the hogs that came in from the forest—a "tolling" calculated to prevent them from "going wild" altogether.

When the morning chores were completed, Harman and his men embarked on their expedition down the Louisa to Vancouver's station. All but Henry Skaggs entered the huge canoe drawn up on the river bank. It had been laboriously carved out of a long poplar log and moved swiftly under a half dozen paddles. The canoe was twenty-four feet long and, in the clutch of a strong current, disappeared around a bend within moments after it was launched.

Two and a half hours later they reached Vancouver's station, a square, massive blockhouse standing on a sandy spit of land. Its base was fashioned of stones piled one upon another to a height of seven feet, with spaces left at intervals for loopholes. The stones, like the round log superstructure, were daubed with clay. The land behind the little bastion and sloping down to the edge of the water had been cleared of trees, bushes and wild cane.

Vancouver's little garrison were delighted to receive visitors. A considerable collection of low-quality summer pelts and stacks of trade goods were stored in the blockhouse. Daily, now, Vancouver's trappers were taking high-grade pelts from animals fattened against the winter, and frames of tanning hides stood about in the sunlight. A half-completed flatboat was tied up at the bank. Vancouver intended to send the pelts down the Sandy to the Ohio and thence to Louisville for shipment to the French in Louisiana. Work on the flatboat stopped and the men spent an hour exchanging stories. As a trader, Vancouver had always maintained good relations with the Indians. His present post was several months old and he had been visited by small bands of Mingoes and Shawnees. He had traded with them, exchanging handfuls of salt, leaden bullets and cotton cloth for the skins of beaver, black bear, deer, foxes, lynx and mountain lions. Vancouver was of the opinion that the Indians had abandoned Sandy Valley and that settlement could proceed in safety. Harman disputed this, pointing out that large Indian nations inhabited the hills and plains of Ohio to the north and the Tennessee hills to the south. He believed the autumn would bring numerous parties into the valley and warned that they were certain to be hostile.

Vancouver opened a five-gallon keg of new whiskey and poured generous draughts of the fiery liquor for all hands—toasting in a soft French accent the future of the Big Sandy Valley. Their appetites whetted by the alcohol, the men ate a heavy meal of venison and corn pone. A similar keg of the spirits was loaded in the canoe. The visitors then took up tools and worked on the ungainly flatboat through the rest of the morning. Using a pit-saw, they fashioned broad, smooth planks which they fastened into place with slender hickory pegs. Noon was two hours past when the last long, clean, poplar board was pegged down. Then, with handshakes and expressions of gratitude all around, Harman's party pushed their clumsy boat onto the river and headed upstream. The river was swollen by heavy rains on its headwaters and the rolling tide struggled against their passage. Though the day had been long and they were tired, the men plied the paddles steadily. At dusk a half-moon shot above the southern hills and lighted the river with wan rays. Like cold imploring ghosts, gargantuan sycamores lifted their white arms along the watercourse. Long before the journey upstream ended, John Skaggs opined that he had come a hell of a long way to get a dram of whiskey.

When they were still miles below their destination the

wind brought a faint whisper of sound to Harman's ears. He held the paddle out of the water and admonished his companions to be silent. "Hark," he said, "do ye hear? Do ye hear?"

The splashing of paddles and the heavy breathing of the men ceased. Impelled by the momentum of the last paddle thrust, the boat moved for a moment upstream, then, while the men sat quietly with their paddles in their hands, began to drift with the current. The borderers looked at one another or stared off into the night. Whatever the sound Harman had heard, none of the others had detected it. After a moment John Skaggs demanded, "What is it, Tice? I didn't hear a thing."

"I'm not shore," said Harman, "but I think it was the ram's horn."

The moments passed, and in the eerie half-light the dugout continued to drift downstream. Only the suppressed breathing of the men and the gentle sighing of the night wind was to be heard. Then down the river on a frail trace of breeze came the sound again, faint and far and hoarse. It was a dying reverberation set off by Martha Draper's ram's-horn trumpet.

"That's it!" said Harman. From that moment the men knew precisely what to do and they did it. They shoved the boat ashore and tied it to a tree. Then, rifles in hand, they moved swiftly and like gray apparitions through the shadows of the night. The ram's horn was a signal the settlers had agreed on long ago to proclaim the presence of Indians and to be sounded for no other purpose. Obviously the little fort had not fallen, but they would have to glean all other information about its condition from the night and the wilderness.

A thousand yards below the fort, they left the valley and climbed a ridge to a rocky point. In the autumn night, the drying leaves rattled and shivered. The moon shed a dimming glow over the harsh and ancient landscape on which was set, like some trifling sore, the diminutive, palisaded cluster of shacks and sheds. Measuring it against the immensity of the wilderness and calculating the strength of the Ohio and Tennessee tribes, the men marveled at the intrepidity that had prompted them to put it there.

The little band moved along the ridge to a flat overlooking the entire valley and the yawning hollow that was the mouth of John's Creek. There they settled, soundless and unmoving, every eye alert for danger, ears straining for unusual noises. For an hour, then two hours, they sat, the night noises shattered and overwhelmed by occasional rasping blasts from the ram's horn. They listened for the suspicious little quirks that might reveal the presence of a hidden foe. There came the howling of wolves, a sound that trailed away into silence as the pack took up the spoor of an animal and disappeared to the south. From beyond the river, high on a huge tree-grown crag, came the deep cough of a mountain lion and from the top of a tall, long-dead chestnut quavered the querulous hooting of an owl. There was a rustle of wings in treetops and, soon to be silenced for the winter, the bellow of bullfrogs from the river. Several times they heard the heart-rending wail of birds and animals caught in the clutches of predators. From time to time, the dogs at the station roused themselves, barking and snarling at some disturbance. Occasionally, they pursued intruding animals far along the hills, and once some of them came to their masters lurking in the shadows on the hillside. The men were witnesses to a score of forest dramas, but in each case the flutter of life rang true. Not even the finely attuned ears of John Skaggs and Tice Harman could detect the faintest counterfeit in any of them. When the moon disappeared over the northern ridges, and a deeper bloom settled over the landscape, a biting chill sank onto the land. The sounds dwindled and died and the wilderness slept. Harman stood up. "Well, men," he said in a low, but positive voice, "Indians have been here. But they're gone. I can smell a redskin, and no matter how damned smart he is with his rascally noises, I can catch'im. But we've not heerd a one of the red devils tonight and they wouldn't have stayed quiet this long. Whatever skeered the women, and I don't doubt that it was Indians, there's no need to be skeered now. But if they are gone, they'll likely come back, and then is when the devil will have to be paid his due!"

Quietly they filed down the hill, and though each of them shared Harman's assessment of the situation, they took no chances. Their rifles were at the ready. Knives were loosened in their leather scabbards. But no warriors materialized out of the white mists. The dogs roused themselves at their approach and barked savagely for a moment before slinking back to their rest. At the edge of the clearing, Harman put his fingers to his mouth and blew softly. A thin low whistle shrilled from his lips. He repeated it three times and, after a brief interval, three times again. As they emerged from the shadows of the forest and drew near the gate, it turned on its huge hinges and they passed within.

The blockhouse was in total darkness except for a faint glow from the banked ashes in the fireplace. The children slept, but the adults were wide awake in an atmosphere tingling with tension. The women surged around the men, questions pouring from their lips. The answers they received were brief and, for the moment at least, reassuring: there were no Indians in the vicinity; of that all were certain.

The men were astounded to hear that Jenny Wiley, their long-lost neighbor, had materialized from the forest beyond the river. The covering of dead ashes was raked back from the hot coals and a new fire was kindled with shavings of chestnut wood. As the flames lighted up the crude interior with its loopholes and rows of bags and barrels, Jenny was led forward to be seen and to retell her story. Harman feasted his eyes upon her. "Jenny, Jenny," he said, "I had long ago give ye up fer lost. Everybody had give ye up'cept Tom Wiley. He has never stopped looking fer ye, and has never doubted that some way or other he would get ye back. As fer me, when the Indians crossed the Louisa with ye, I lost hope that we would ever see ye again unless the red devils took ye to Canada fer ransom, or some miracle took place. Ye are a right smart woman, Jenny, and a credit to Hezekiah Sellards and to all his blood and line." Smoke from his stubby corncob pipe wreathed his wrinkled face and eddied about his yellow beard and strange, faded eyes. "Ye lived with them wicked red varmin for a year and then got clean away from them, and that is a miracle, to be sure."

Food was prepared and set before the hungry men. Jenny had eaten supper a few hours before, but she sat at the table and ate again. After existing for a year on Indian food, the sweet taste of milk, butter and cornbread rolled on her tongue like honey. And while they ate she recounted all her adventures with the Indians from the sudden onslaught against her cabin to the moment when the blockhouse gate shut behind her. When Jenny's story had been heard in all its grim details, the men sat staring into the fire, quietly smoking their pipes. At last Henry Skaggs observed, "That pair of red snakes, the Shawnees and the Cherokees, have been raiding the settlements for a long time. The Cherokee is a cousin—some say a half-brother—of Benge, and he's just as savage as Benge and maybe worse. He's a bloodthirsty devil and someday somebody will tan his hide fer a saddle blanket. A few years ago he hit the settlements on the Cheat River and the militiamen who went there could tell it was old Cap'n John's work by the way he took no prisoners. He killed the settlers as he come to 'em, burning the wounded alive in their own cabins."

Skaggs paused and puffed his pipe. "But the Shawnee, now, is another matter. He's old and sly. He's a human fox. He's a lot older than you might have guessed him to be, Jenny. I'm seventy-six and he mought be nearly as old as I am, not quite, but nearly. He's like an old fox; he can still run fast. So far he's kept ahead of the hounds. For years during the Revolution and before, he was in the service of the British and they trusted him a mighty lot. I've heerd it said on good report that he was one of the Indians who drawed a British officer's pay and carried a sword. Someday the Cherokee will get his just deserts. I have no doubt of that. But now, old Black Wolf, he's like his namesake—he's run at the head of his pack fer a long, long time and I think he'll keep on a-gettin' away. Time'll get him, but I doubt that any white man's bullet ever will."

Harman swore an emphatic oath. "I'm 'fraid ye're 'bout right, Henry. Ye've sized'em up the way I would. They're both dangerous as cocked guns, but the Shawnee is the sly one, now. He's sneaky, he's smart, he knows both white men and Indians and the ways of both. And he's patient, aye patient as death. He's a dangerous man to have agin ye, and a man to be afeared of!"

A long silence ensued, then Harman looked at Jenny, a smile twinkling about the corners of his bearded lips. "Jenny," he said, "we're mighty glad to see ye back and I guess yer husband will be the happiest man in Virginia when we get ye to him. He's roamed these old valleys fer months tryin' to find some trace o'ye, and ye know he's no woodsman and probably wouldn't a' recognized yer track if he had come across it. Tom's a brave man and a good man but you ain't home to him yet. The savages will try their best to get ye agin long afore ye get to Walker's Valley. A lot of people have come in from the East and settled there in the last year, but old Cap'n John will be so put out at losing ye that he may attack the settlement anyway. When ye get home ye and Tom will have to be mighty careful all the time or ye'll wind up an Indian squaw atter all, and this time fer keeps. We've been here half a year now, stuck up like a pimple on a man's nose, and the savages have been about from time to time, 'cause we've seen signs o' them, but till now they've never bothered us. They've been off in the mountains somewhere doing God knows what. But now that ye're here, Jenny, they'll send to the Ohio territory and to the Tennessee for more bucks and they'll attack this place, probably in enough strength to burn it down and kill us all. If we stay, we'll be attacked during the winter. And that's not the worst part of it. We'll be besieged. They'll surround the place and try to starve us out if they can't burn us out.

"And if we leave, they'll come in behind us and burn the fort and all the buildings we've put up this summer. All will go up in smoke within a day after we pull out of here. And on our way back they're apt to ambush us. Indians have a way o' gettin' signals from one place to another. I don't know how they do it, but they can get the word around when a conclave is wanted. There may be half a dozen other bands skulking around somewhere in these mountains between the Ohio and the Cumberland and all of them may close in on us within a few days. If they attack us on the trail, we'll be in a right bad fix. But we've fought our way out o' other scrapes and we can fight our way out agin. We may take some scalps, but we're not a-goin' to lose yer'n takin' ye home." And with an affirmative shake of his head that dispelled all doubt, he declared, "And they ain't a-goin' to git ye back agin, either, whether they's twelve o' 'em or thirty or a hundred.

"We'd better leave somebody as a lookout and to wake us up if the dogs git riled, and the rest had better git to sleep, because we've gota lot o'work to do laid out afore we leave here."

Some voices of dissent were raised against Harman's proposal to abandon the fort. The women, especially, were pessimistic about surrendering the results of months of hard toil. To return to the older settlements now would spell the loss of fields and fences, the blockhouse, and a half-dozen lesser structures.

Aquila Harman, Tice's nephew, put forward the suggestion that a party be dispatched to escort Jenny back to her home while the others remained behind to defend the fort, but the fallacy of this course was apparent. There were scarcely enough people in the settlement to defend the walls when all were present. If even a few of the rifles were sent away, the place would be doomed and Jenny would be subjected to the horror of recapture if her guards were overtaken by a considerable band.

The little circle of people sat in complete silence for

several moments, light from the flames flickering over their features and comforting them with its warmth. Pain, disappointment, and anger stirred in the hard-eyed men and weary-faced women, and in the solemn boys and girls sobered far beyond their years by the cruel and bloodstained environment in which they had spent their brief lives. But things like this happened on the frontier. Men were killed. Women and children were slaughtered or carried away into the lodges of savages. Houses were burned. The accumulations of years of patient and incredibly hard labor were consumed in flames. Such heartbreaking experiences had been familiar to them all their lives and to their forebears, neighbors and friends for decades. As they looked into the future, they could not visualize a time when the grim dangers through which they passed would be lifted from their hearths. The luxury of a night's sleep undisturbed by the horrifying possibility of a merciless onslaught by hate-filled warriors was unthinkable to them. Most had never known such luxury. Horror and hardship had conditioned them to bear practically any affliction and to sustain an implacable appetite for vengeance on the red curse that clouded their lives.

Henry Skaggs broke the silence to tell Jenny about the life Tom Wiley had lived after the obliteration of his family. And though she had held back her tears through a year-long captivity, she wept with her face cradled in her hands as the old backwoodsman described her husband's unceasing search for her and his patient reconstruction of their shattered home.

"Jenny, Tom was almost crushed by grief when he got home that night about midnight and found his house hollowed out by fire and ye and his baby gone and all of his other young'uns dead. But he behaved like a good solid man. He didn't break down. He and John Borders went fer help but most of the men were away huntin', as ye well know, but then he got a few men and boys together, with muskets and old rifles. They went back to yer place and searched around and made shore ye was gone and that the Indians had left. Then they took off lookin' fer ye. He reckoned they was Cherokees and had gone down the New River toward their infernal towns, but of course he never found nothing— not a sign nor a track.

"While they was gone the rest of the boys and the women dug graves on the little p'int to the east above yer house and buried yer brother and children. And each one had a coffin, too. Enough was rounded up in the settlement to bury them all, but the two littlest 'uns was laid together in the same box.

"Tom has carved each one a tombstone and in the spring when the wild flowers are bloomin' and the laurel is dark green on the hill below them, there can't be any prettier graveyard in the world. It's a proper place fer Christian dead to lay in.

"Later, Tom sent off a letter to Williamsburg and got the governor to write the Canadian governor at Detroit to have a lookout made fer ye and to post a ransom fer ye. Then he went off by hisself and hunted through these hills fer weeks, and all the way to the Ohio. He passed the Painted Licks and one night he slept under a cliff where ye had spent a night, bekase he saw yer foot track plain in the dust by the ashes of an old cold fire. But the big river was in full tide and he found no other trace o'ye. When he got back he said, `My Jenny had vanished clear away like mist burnt off by the sun.'

"Anyway, he never did give ye up fer lost and he never will, if I know Tom Wiley. He has built the house back as good as new. When ye get home ye'll miss yer children mightily, o'course, but ye'll be pleased to find so much built back and as fine a man as this country holds a-waitin' to see ye agin."

Later as she lay down on a pallet in a corner she wept anew with gratitude that so much was left to her out of the ruins of her past life—her husband, her home, her health and the chance, however hard, to begin anew.

The fort was astir by daylight. Under the leadership of Harman and John Skaggs, eleven men went out and scouted the ridges overlooking the valley and the trails along the creek banks. Finding no indication that the outpost was under surveillance, they followed Jenny's directions to the rockhouse on Little Mud Lick. They hoped to end the danger to their settlement by closing with the savages and destroying them before their numbers could be swollen by new recruits, but their foray was fruitless. The ashes of the campfire were cold and the shelter was abandoned. The tracks of the departing warriors had been carefully concealed, indicating that they had dispersed. Skaggs looked down from the cliff at the field where Jenny had toiled so long and so patiently and spat tobacco juice in disappointment and frustration. "Gone, damn'em, since midnight or before! Gone atter their redassed heathen kinfolks as shore as hell is hot!" Then almost pensively, "With women and children to look atter, we ain't seen the last of 'em yet, and ye can bank on that."

When they returned to the mouth of John's Creek, every possibility of attack was guarded against, notwithstanding the clear evidence that they were in no immediate danger. All that afternoon and through the following day men patrolled the riverbanks and the hill crests while others prepared for the southward trek.

The little herd of cattle was driven in. The hogs were simply turned loose in the hope that when the settlers returned, perhaps in the following spring, some of the animals could be rounded up. At best they could hope that a few could avoid the fangs and talons of wolves, bears, and mountain lions and bobcats. The cows were fitted with halters for leading if they began to lag behind. The little stock of corn was shelled and sacked. Small children and three pregnant women were assigned places on horses and mules. Other animals would carry bags of shelled corn, dried meat, salt, stores of lead and gunpowder, clothing and household "plunder."

Jenny spent a third night at the fort. Then at sunrise the little caravan moved out. Tice Harman rode in advance, his huge long-barreled rifle across the pommel of his saddle. He rode the same great, tall stallion that had carried him in such close pursuit of Jenny's abductors a year earlier.

Another man on horseback followed Harman. Then came the women and children, with two men bringing up the rear. The other men walked a hundred yards or so away from the caravan on its flanks or scouted along the ridges to the fore. All were superlative infantry soldiers. Most of them had never had a moment of military training except the highly informal muster drills of the border militia, and while they were not soldierly they were extremely warlike. At all costs, they would avoid a surprise attack on their flanks, rear or front, and prevent the savages from reaching their women and children. Accompanied by their dogs, they instinctively probed groves of trees, clumps of laurel, moss-grown boulders and patches of cane. And though they startled deer and foxes and strings of wild turkeys, and caused multitudes of squirrels to chatter excitedly as they passed, they saw no trace of their real quarry—the pernicious red people who had tracked these hills for thousands of years.

Where the trail was broad and clear the horses moved with considerable speed, but the men on foot and the plodding women and children did not fall behind. Harman saw to that. From time to time he held the horses back, slowing them often enough to keep pace with the slowest of his company. Occasionally he climbed down from the saddle and walked beside his horse. Occasionally he left the trail entirely and, leaving his horse to be ridden by one of the women or girls, clambered to a rocky spur to gaze intently into the next valley. Each time the party crossed a ridge, dividing one valley from another, they carefully studied the wilderness landscape, selecting from years of experience the places where their foes were most likely to lie in wait for them.

The winding trail up John's Creek was broad and clear and they moved at a steady clip, slowed occasionally when they followed lesser trails across jutting ridges in order to avoid skirting them and fording rushing streams. Harman knew the way well. He and the Skaggs brothers had traveled it many times, alone or together. They knew that the John's Creek trace led with remarkable directness to the Great Laurel Ridge and beyond, where a prong veered eastward toward Walker's Mountain; and that by following it and moving rapidly they might reach the older settlement and its riflemen before their adversaries could gather for an assault. But the upper reaches of that trace led through low, wild country where the caravan would be almost impossible to defend and where an attack would be disastrous. This they would avoid even at the cost of fording a savage creek or two and climbing some extremely precipitous slopes.

As the hours passed without incident or alarm, the tension lessened and the march slowed a little. The walking women and children were allowed turns in the saddles and the cattle were permitted to graze on trailside grasses and in scattered cane patches. But they did not halt until starlit darkness overtook them in a windy gap where they camped under a shallow cliff. They allowed themselves the luxury of a low fire but screened it carefully to lessen its light. Like the Indians, Jenny's new companions stirred early and the harried people and their bawling cattle were on the trail again long before the trailing mist lifted from the path.

Another day and another night slipped behind as the trail climbed upward with the rising land, then shifted to the southwest along ridges, through gaps and along benches studded with gigantic beech trees and laurel thickets. The course they followed would add many miles to their return to Walker's Creek but would enable them to avoid the broken hills, tumbled boulders and tangled canebrakes on the upper limits of the Tug—a place made to order for ambush.

In the afternoon after a long ascent the animals were winded and a halt was ordered under an overhanging ledge. Jenny laid her rifle across her lap, closed her eyes and leaned back against the scaly bark of a fallen hickory. As her weary limbs and nerves relaxed she heard vicious snarls and barks from one of the dogs on the hillside above her. As she opened her eyes and sat upright there was a wild rustling of leaves and an exclamation from one of the women. A black and white bundle of canine affection and joy leaped into her lap. She was knocked backward and flattened as a delirious

Tige licked her hands and face, whining and barking in a tail-wagging frenzy of happiness.

With much difficulty Jenny managed to calm the creature. At last after a final vigorous sniff he settled down in her lap to have his head stroked and his ears pulled. Her happiness at the reunion was almost as great as his own. In the hardest days of her captivity, he had been her only friend and comforter, sharing her bed and morsels of food. She was certain that there had been times when, without his friendship and sympathy, she would have slipped over the abyss into insanity. She had last seen him at the heels of Dull Knife and his appearance now signaled that at least some of the savages were nearby.

Of course there was a possibility that the animal had left the warriors and struck off into the forest on his own in quest for his mistress. But they knew, also, of the fondness of Indians for dogs. Their towns teemed with mongrels and they sometimes accompanied them on their wilderness sojourns. Henry Skaggs scowled down at the little animal and spat tobacco juice between his brown, snaggly teeth. "That damn Cherokee is nigh, Jenny. He could be lookin' at ye right now, fer that matter!"

But another night passed without an alarm and a new day found the party watchful and worried, certain now that the issue of Jenny's freedom and their survival would be decided by arms somewhere on the trail ahead.

Heavy rains fell during the night and streams swelled to turbulent serpents of water. Frost had fallen two or three times and leaves, loosened by cold and rioting in every conceivable color, were falling by the millions. Moccasins and hooves sank in a rustling carpet of brown, gold, green, red, yellow, orange, and purple. The retreating settlers passed gigantic stones that had weathered from the rock-crested mountains and come to rest by the stream. Rounded and smoothed by time, coated with moss and capped with ferns and scrub pines, they lay half submerged in the foaming water. The narrowing bottoms were rank with wild cane and the soil, nurtured by countless generations of close-growing stalks, was black as coal and many feet deep. Horses wandering off the beaten track sank to their fetlocks in the yielding loam.

The whole length of the trail was marked by death. Bones strewn about like beads testified to the violence of the struggles that raged by day and night within the wilderness. At fords the skulls of deer, elk, and buffalo glittered like chunks of chalk along the shallow water. Bits of fur from rabbits, squirrels, and raccoons, too, told of prey and hunter. Again, the sweetish stench of decaying flesh and the flapping of the gray wings of vultures marked the demise of some forest creature.

Countless wild things sprang from before them and fled across the hillsides. From the mouth of a cane-choked hollow, a bull buffalo and a small herd of cows and calves looked at them with mild wonder in their rounded dark eyes. A spotted doe bounded from a beech grove and with prodigious leaps disappeared amid the trees. A fat and glossy black bear lay on an overhanging rock and fished with a claw-tipped paw for small catfish swimming in a deep pool. Aroused by the barking of the dogs, he struggled to his feet, gazed at the intruders for a moment, and waddled into a thicket. Turkeys scurried through the forest gobbling and drumming with huge wings. A rattlesnake gave imperious warning from a crevice at the base of a cliff, then slithered back into the darkness. Packs of curious wolves followed them by day and ringed their camp at night, filling the darkness with blood-curling howls and snarls. Foxes barked their taunting challenge to the dogs from crags and thickets and the drumming of pheasants resounded hollowly from coves and ridge tops.

Once, for many hours, a sea of life whirred and roared across the heavens above them. Tens of millions of gray passenger pigeons flying southward blotted out the sun and shrouded the land in somber shadow.

Nor were any of these sights unusual or surprising. The older men had been drawn into the wilderness by the immensity of its animal resources and the richness of its agricultural possibilities. The children, born in the shadows of the great trees, accepted the tremendous vitality of the forest as a matter of course, eternal and inexhaustible. The mountains were a kindly environment, affording shelter against bitter winds and containing countless caverns and cliffs where wild creatures could find refuge from storms. The rich mast blanketed the earth with brown nuts of many varieties and the creatures that devoured them and were devoured, in turn, by other creatures caused the land to rustle and stir and start with an energy as unresting as waves on a sea beach.

On the third day, after they had passed beyond the headwaters of John's Creek, the trail ascended sharply to climb the steep face of the Great Laurel Ridge—a long spine known today as the Pine Mountain. As they veered southward they approached the "Hollow Mountain"—a deep chasm chiseled through the ridge by the rushing waters of a fork of the Louisa and called by later generations the "Breaks of the Big Sandy." On either side, sheer sandstone cliffs jutted grim and gray like the walls of colossal castles seventeen hundred feet above the sparkling river. The canyon was a perfect place for an ambush, offering attackers numerous well-concealed vantage points from which to fire down on a foe. Consequently, they avoided the trail that ran like a fine thread beside the riverbank and pursued a path Henry Skaggs called "Nemicolon's Trace," after a Delaware warchief whose warriors had followed it to the astonishing victory against General Braddock. It forded the stream and snaked like a filament of gossamer across the rocky face of the ridge. Up, up, up the little caravan climbed, people and animals pulling themselves along dim paths and sometimes, where there were no paths at all, between mammoth poplars and limestone boulders. In a remote geologic cataclysm, the earth's crust had buckled, thrusting up a vast wrinkle extending more than a hundred miles to the southwest. In the process, the rending limestone lifted out of the depths of the earth was thrust to the northward, shattering and piling up in immense quantities on the northern slope of the new ridge. Sweetened by the dissolving lime, the soil supported the largest trees in the southern Appalachians. Even the forest-wise Harman paused to gaze in amazement at some of them. On the flat bench, where the black loam lay deep between heaps of stones, tulip trees cast shadows ten feet across and soared straight up for fifty yards.

As the sun sank a little from the high of noon, they reached the crest of the ridge and stood on a massive ledge of sun-baked sandstone dotted at intervals with gnarled and twisted pines. Here the little band rested briefly before beginning their descent of the southern slope.

Awestruck, Jenny looked down into the yawning canyon. The river tumbled through the mountain, roaring over the rock-strewn bed, swirling in angry cascades, then rippling over sandy shallows before plunging against new obstructions. The turbulent passage reverberated from the cliffs in a hollow roar, sometimes muffled as the wind changed and again booming like distant thunder.

Then she looked to the northwest into the tangled hills of her year-long captivity and was overwhelmed anew. The hills and valleys of the Appalachian heartland lay like the frozen waves of a gigantic and berserk ocean. Turbulent, vast, savage, ancient, the sea extended in a mighty arc from the base of Great Laurel Ridge as far as the eye could carry, and everywhere, from the creeks to the rocky crests, there soared a choking carpet of trees.

On the lower slopes, the poplars stood tall and imperious, fringed by columns of silvery sycamores and dark druidical hemlocks. On the higher land were endless groves of chestnuts, oaks, maples, basswoods, hornbeams, hickories and beeches. Red oaks, chestnut oaks and patches of ivy and rhododendron crowded about the huge sandstone crests which time had carved into weird columns, arches, and towers. And the whole flamed with all the exotic colors of autumn.

Though Jenny did not know it, she was gazing upon one of the oldest forests in the world, with its roots going back in the same soil for seventy million years, a woodland that had survived countless cataclysms to reseed eastern America time after time. In the icy eons when the trees had died or were buried beneath glaciers on the great plains and along the eastern seacoast, the Appalachians sheltered their forests against the day when new cycles would melt the ice and invite the growth of trees again. Then by rivers and winds these ancient hills had sent forth their seeds to replant the barren and ravaged land on two great continents.

Soon men would come with oxen, mules, and horses, with cattle and droves of hogs, with rifles, axes, and fires, and with tough-willed women and gangs of irrepressible children. In their zest for life and conquest, they would challenge the majesty and dignity of the wilderness and destroy them and reduce the age-old forest to a pitiable remnant. But Jenny could foresee none of this as she stood humbled by the gigantic spectacle and heard the autumn wind whisper of impending winter.

CHAPTER SIXTEEN

In midafternoon the procession left the trail and, with Harman in the lead, passed through a laurel thicket and ascended a broad ridge to camp for the night under a deep shelving cliff. The crisp weather was excellent for travel, but Harman inspected the place with a finality that showed they would go no farther that day.

The cliff was thirty yards long and at its deepest extended thirty feet into the sandstone. The top arched like a great shell a dozen feet above the sandy floor. Round kettle-stones had fallen and lay along the outer edge of the shelter. At the back, oblong slabs had split off from the sandstone ledge and were ranged like immense stone coffins in a ragged row. Harman beckoned to the men and outlined his strategy to them.

Drawing vigorously on his pipe and combing his yellow beard with the callused fingers of his left hand, he opined, "We're a-goin' to see redskins afore mornin', and here is about as good a place as I know of in these mountains fer us to see 'em." The broad hand at the end of the short, slender arm gestured down the hill toward the game trace and the stubby thumb jabbed toward the thin stand of trees that extended for three hundred yards down the hill. The incline was gentle and in some places almost flat. Three or four acres were dotted with small beeches and pines. Beyond that dense laurel fringed oaks and hemlocks.

"Hit's almost certain that the Cherokee and his men set an ambush fer us down in the badlands in that gorge back yander. They waited and waited, expectin' us to come any minute. And if we had come, in the Hollow Mountain there they would have jumped us, we'd have had the battle of our lives. By now they've discovered that we ain't a-comin' and they'll know exactly what's happened. They'll head out of the gorge and find us and afore nightfall they'll be here. Now here's what me and Henry think ought to be done. We want to see whether it meets with what you men and women think is right. We can't give no orders, but we've had a lot of experience with Indians—more than any of the rest o'ye, unless it's Jenny. We think our plan is the best way to handle the devils.

"Ye see these fallen rocks back here. There's plenty of 'em to hide every man here. I want us men to get down behind 'em and out of sight with our guns loaded and ready. I want you women to set up the camp. Drag in some wood. There's plenty of it in sight right here. Build a fire and start cooking supper. Keep the dogs out in front and when the Indians come they'll bark and be uneasy. When the savages scout the place they'll look fer us and they won't see a man anywhere. They'll wait awhile and get mighty curious and mystified. We hope they will decide that the men have all gone off to hunt or out to try to ambush them. They'll scout fer us and not find us, then they'll make a headlong rush fer Jenny and, likely, some of the other women and children, too. Keep a sharp lookout and when your back is turned, look fer 'em with yer ears. If we men lay real quiet and completely out of sight, they'll finally decide that we're not here, and when the redskins come after Jenny we'll git 'em. Ye see," he pointed again," the timber is too small to hide anybody afore he gits to the thicket. When they charge we'll git 'em and when they run away, we'll git 'em agin!"

He looked steadfastly at Jenny for a long moment and then his strange, almost colorless eyes swept from face to face, probing each for doubt or approval. Henry Skaggs cleared his throat. "Jenny, ye're bait," he said. "Ye're a sheep set up to draw the wolves and ye will be sacrificed if the plan goes sour. We want ye to pick out a big rock and put yer rifle behind it, and when the red rascals come in sight ye can get a crack at 'em. Hit's a chancy thing but the best way out if we don't flinch and have jest a grain o' luck."

After a moment one of the men ventured, "The snakefaces may believe we air out a-huntin' them and that they have found the camp with the men all gone. Goddamn! They'll charge as shore as hell is hot. They want Jenny alive and will come in atter the women with their hatchets instead of shootin' at them." He smiled in pleasant contemplation of the possibilities.

A long silence ensued, broken only by the low breathing of the people ranged in a circle under the cliff. Then one of the men picked up his rifle and gear and climbed behind a slab of sandstone, pulling himself down completely out of sight. Within a moment or two the last of the men was hidden. The women called the dogs out into the semiclearing beyond the cliff and commenced the task of making camp.

Throughout the discussion, the children who were old enough to comprehend the situation listened with wide-eyed attentiveness. None interrupted or asked a question, but when the plan was agreed upon by the adults all immediately made themselves available to contribute to its success. The red warriors were the psychological scourge of backwoods children and they knew from countless blood-curdling tales the gruesome fate likely to be theirs if they fell into the Indians' hands.

The women and children dragged in fallen branches, venturing several hundred yards away to get the fuel. They spread down buffalo hides and blankets of hard, home-woven wool. As the sun descended they lighted a fire and flames leaped up to give welcome heat against the advancing chill.

Jenny helped them bring firewood to the shelter and carried pails of water from a shallow stream a hundred yards away. Like the other women and the older children she struggled to maintain her composure and to appear calm and unafraid, but her heart pounded in her ears like a hammer and more than once her head swam dizzily from excitement and dread.

Near the middle of the shelter, a slab of sandstone shielded an area ten feet long and about six feet wide. There blankets were spread down and the five suckling babies were cradled on blankets, and two girls were designated to care for them. The other children—those too young to bear arms of any sort—were instructed that at the first onslaught they were to flee to this protected space and to remain there until the attack ended. Older children were charged with responsibility for the younger ones.

When they had chopped the firewood for the camp, the women leaned their keen axes within easy reach. The adolescent boys were handed rifles, powder horns and bullets and given positions to defend.

As an hour and then another wore on the tension mounted inexorably. The nerves of the women drew as tight as bowstrings and their eyes strayed through the trees and the rhododendron thicket. Their ears were alert for footfalls or the signaling cries of birds and beasts—cries almost, but not quite, genuine.

Suddenly the calm was broken. A dog lying on a carpet of brown leaves a dozen paces from the fire sprang to his feet with a deep roaring growl. Others followed suit, and in seconds were ranged in a snarling half-circle facing outward from the shelter. A huge black and brown mastiff advanced to the middle of the clearing and stood with rear legs outstretched and head lowered, drooling saliva between savage barks. One or two of the more timid beasts slunk backward, their tails low, to find shelter among the women.

Then suddenly, and in silence, Indians broke from the cover of the thicket. Running low and fast they sprang over the leaf-strewn forest floor. In her first sweeping glance Jenny estimated that there were a dozen or more of them. Each carried a rifle in one hand and a tomahawk or knife in the other. Polly Anderson dropped a piece of wood she was dragging into the fire and bounded toward her axe, shrieking, "Injuns! Injuns! Lord, ha' mercy on us! Injuns!"

The cry was taken up by several of the others. The emotions which gripped Jenny froze her vocal cords. She sprang to her rifle but never once took her eyes from a sturdy, stocky figure in frayed leather breeches and a faded blue shirt and jacket. Brown and white eagle feathers were bound in his black hair and a blue scarf encircled his forehead. In his hair, a few pieces of silver glittered in the dying sunlight.

Within seconds the savages had covered half the distance. Suddenly hoarse and bloodthirsty masculine cries resounded from the rocky walls and a line of leather-shirted woodsmen sprang up along the ragged row of fallen rocks, each gripping a long and awkward-looking Pennsylvania muzzle-loader. At the startling and wholly unexpected spectacle, the Indians broke into yells and some of them hesitated for a fatal instant. Then they bounded for the shelter of trees, but not before the rifles had cracked in a hollow, booming volley. Black-powder smoke eddied above the rocks, spiralling upward into the gathering gloom. Frantically the men rammed new charges of powder, patches and balls into the smoking throats of their rifles. Four of the braves lay perfectly still and a fifth writhed in the dust, his spine severed by a bullet. While the hickory ramrods clicked against the metal, the others sped to the edge of the clearing. A last shot from Andrew Draper's rifle plowed with a thud into the back of a fleeing skull. The warrior's knees buckled, his rifle and hatchet clattered from his hands, and he slid face downward into the leaves. A ball struck another sprinting brave near the elbow and he disappeared into the thicket with a tremulous howl.

The attack was over in seconds. From the first warning bark to the last shot scarcely sixty seconds elapsed. Five Indians were dead and another lay dying before them. Dull Knife, the Cherokee, was not among the fallen, but he had not escaped unmarked.

When Jenny seized her rifle she whirled with the piece already at her shoulder. Dull Knife was thirty yards away and disbelief, bewilderment, and wrath flared across his brown features. In that flickering moment the Cherokee measured the full extent of the devastating ambush into which he had stumbled and his face mirrored all the incredulity and frustration an outmarshaled warrior can feel in the clutches of a craftier foe.

The muscular form leaped behind an eighteen-inch beech, the volley rang out, and a bullet sent a piece of white bark spinning from the tree. With scarcely a pause Dull Knife sprang into the open again, dodging evasively from tree to tree before another withering blast could catch him. As he left the shelter of the tree, the side of his face was turned toward her and Jenny caught him in her sights and squeezed the hair trigger. As the rifle slammed against her shoulder, the Cherokee lurched and stumbled, then almost instantly regained his momentum. But in a split second after the fire and smoke flashed from her rifle barrel, Jenny saw a deep red welt spin across his forehead.

With curses and taunting cries the white men pursued them, but the Indians had lost all heart for the conflict. Spatters of blood reddened scattered leaves and beds of moss. In a half-hour the men returned satisfied that, as one of them phrased it, "The redskins have took off like scalded dogs."

And, indeed, they had been scalded by a bungled, headlong rush into disaster. As Jenny reloaded her rifle, Mahala Hawes crushed the skull of the fallen warrior. As the axe fell in a vicious coup de grace, Jenny recognized the cruel and vindictive features of Red Turtle, the Mingo torturer.

Some of the men squatted by the savages and with deft fingers and keen knives took their scalps. Repelled by the spectacle and by the horrid memories the act sledge-hammered into her mind, she turned her back and covered her face with her hands. For the last time, she heard the tearing of flesh and tissue as the dead Mingo underwent the supreme indignity. Then boys seized the bodies by the heels and dragged them a short distance from the camp where they were left as meat for wolves and vultures.

Henry Skaggs came in and, "hunkering" by the fire, ate copiously of cornbread and venison. As he chewed, he declared, "We have seen the last of the redskins fer a long time. Ye know, Indians are a bloodthirsty lot and they will nuss a grudge fer a mighty long time. When they attack, they're all fire and tow, and their hearts are in it. They don't play around and they mean business, and they don't scare easy. But an Indian disapp'ints easy. When he's been thrashed, he loses heart in a hurry and the fight goes out o' him. He loses faith in his own self and a long time will pass afore he's ready to fight agin. Then he gradually builds up his nerve and comes back. Indians are a lot like children. When they've been whipped, ye don't hear much out of 'em fer a while and these Indians have been whipped real good."

A vigil was maintained through the night, but the camp and its dogs and picketed mules and horses slept undisturbed. Jenny alone could not rest. She lay on a pallet on the sandy ground in a little space between the face of the ancient, moss-grown cliff and a huge slab of stone. She was wrapped in blankets and a nearby fire cast strange flickering shapes onto the rock above her face. For the first time in a year she felt safe. Every exhausting experience she had endured since her captivity began rose before her eyes and raced through her mind. The muscles in her arms and legs tied themselves into hard knots. And she was cold despite the wraps and the flames. Again and again she saw the startled face of Dull Knife, the mouth open, the eyes wide, doom and frustration etched deep in every feature. She saw the red welt lace his forehead as the bullet touched him. She saw him lurch and run, and endlessly she remembered her murdered children and brother, the long excruciating marches, the incredible hours of toil, the unspeakable death of the young man at the stake. And though Tige licked her hand with his coarse tongue and snuggled close to her, she could not relax even for an instant. The long accumulation of tensions pushed against her ribs like uncoiling steel springs, and inside her pounding skull like torrents of plunging water. When at daybreak the sentinel yelled to awaken them she rose as alert and taut as when she had first lain down.

In a day or two she would reach Walker's Creek and all that remained of her family—her husband and the graveyard. But much of Jenny lay beyond the dark western hills where, with her own hands, she had scooped a shallow grave for one of her children and had left the battered form of another as prey for scavengers. She could find no way to escape that dreadful moment at the great sycamore when Dull Knife had dropped her child. Like an etching on glass she saw again and again the flattened form as the storm lifted the edges of the garment in which it was wrapped. Soon she would again be in the arms of Tom Wiley and sit by a warm fire at his hearth. Someday she might find peace again and see the implacable faces of red warriors recede into the shadows of the fleeting years, shedding into those lengthening shadows the smell of scorched meat by open campfires, the weariness of long treks and the degradation she had worn as a white squaw. Time might heal these soul-searing hurts and restore her to passion and womanhood again, but on this morning she was drained empty and her soul was formless and void. But even as she took up the trail to the east across the foothills of the Big Stone Ridge some vague but overpowering impulse whispered that her destiny lay amid the foreboding hills behind her where she had suffered captivity and despair.

A scout went out before dawn and raced far ahead of the plodding column to carry word of their coming to Walker's Creek. His feet lightened by the eagerness of the news-bearer, he sped to the settlement, heading first to the lonely cabin of Tom Wiley. He found the Irishman on a hilltop gazing pensively across the dusk-dimmed maze that had swallowed his wife. His thoughts were on the gentler hills of his boyhood and the strange destiny that had brought him to these wild solitudes and cost him so much here. While fully aware of the dreadful perils inherent in such an undertaking, he had resolved to strike off on a new quest for his lost Jennie—a furtive trip down the Big Sandy and across the Ohio. If by great stealth and daring he could find her without being captured himself, he would then confront the gargantuan task of bringing her home. To find a means of communicating with her, or arranging her escape and protecting her against at least a score of relentless pursuers would require all the ingenuity of a Daniel Boone or a Simon Kenton. No one knew better his limitations as a scout, but as the anniversary of his wife's abduction approached, the poignancy of his grief grew on him anew and he was willing to endure any fate rather than face the future without her.

Within minutes after Peter Harman had poured out his tidings, Tom Wiley was on the hunters' trace the settlers must follow to their old homes. Nor did he leave his saddle or lean his long rifle against the ground through the cool, starlit night. When a pack of a dozen wolves howled on his scent he ignored them, even when their eyes glowed like orbs of fire in the gloomy forest behind him. Puzzled and outraged by his indifference, they pursued him until he strode into the firelight of an awakening camp and clasped his wife to his bosom.

For a long interval man and wife looked at each other while the men, women and children stared in silence or turned respectfully away. The flickering light played over his taut features and the flecks of gray in his reddish hair. It fell on her sun-browned skin and black braids, and on the tears that welled into their eyes. Then her arms went around his waist in a long embrace and before their lips could meet she murmured in a voice drained of all emotions except love and hopefulness, "O Tom, Tom Wiley! I have come back to ye! I have come home again!"

CHAPTER SEVENTEEN

On the farm at Walker's Creek, Tom and Jenny Wiley took up again the threads of their torn lives, weaving them into a single inseparable strand. And the new life, despite its tragic memories, was remarkably composed and free of bitterness.

In Jenny's absence the farm had prospered. The house had acquired a new roof and the interior walls were coated with whitewash. When he had explored and exhausted every hope of recovering his abducted wife and child, Tom had returned to his land. Using labor as a sedative, he toiled to escape from his grief or, rather, to render it more tolerable. In six months of ceaseless labor he carved new fields out of the wilderness and raised new sheds and a barn.

In their reunion they were held together by an immeasurable and inexpressible bond. The loss of four children instilled in each a poignant and understanding compassion for the other. But in a sense they were strangers, too. When the man and woman saw each other again the first time they contrasted starkly—Jenny in a mixture of deerskin and cheap trade garments from Vancouver's stores, tanned and hardened by a year of toil and captivity, and her husband worn and stooped, with a haggard light in his eyes. There was a dreadful year to tell one another about, but after the first telling they seldom spoke of it again. They felt too deeply to rely on words for their expression and, as the years passed, out of their love and loyalty the Wiley family was born again. Jenny was thirty when her sojourn in the wilderness ended, and in the decade that followed six more children were born to them—four sons and two daughters.

Jenny and her husband lived in dread that the grim Cherokee would return, and at night when the wind whistled at the eaves of their cabin and moaned through the trees on the hilltops they listened for his footfalls. For years the calling of night birds and the barking of dogs brought them up awake and tensed to fight for their lives. But if Captain John ever returned, his mission was furtive and harmless. One morning after a light snowfall Tom came into the house and with alarm on his face reported that he had found moccasined footprints near the sheep pen. When Jenny looked at them she shuddered. She had seen the print of that broad and resolute foot many times and had no doubt of its maker. The sun melted the snow quickly and efforts to pursue the skulker were fruitless. Whatever his identity and purpose he never returned.

And in the decade from 1790 to 1800 the land around Walker's Mountain changed. Families pushed in from the Carolina and Virginia Piedmont, from the Shenandoah, out of Pennsylvania and Maryland and Europe. They came steadily—English, Scotch, Irish, German, a scattering of Hollanders. And always the tide of humanity rolled westward. The vast territory between Walker's Valley and the older settlements in the Shenandoah filled with people. A cabin smoked on almost every creek. Worn by the wheels of wagons and the hooves of pack trains, crude roads began to lace the hills and valleys. And the larger game disappeared.

As the land toward the sunrise was tamed and broken, the frontiersmen whom Jenny and Tom had long known and trusted, and many of the newcomers who now dwelt among them, looked with growing hunger on the new lands to the west and north—in the Big Sandy Valley, along the tortuous watershed of the Kentucky and beyond to the plains of the Ohio and Indiana. Harman and his followers went early to rebuild their station on the bottom between the close-set hills above the Painted Licks, and this time they stayed.

As the little backwoodsman had anticipated, the Indians burned the blockhouse within a week after the settlers returned to Walker's Mountain. Nor did they stop there. Bands from Ohio and the Tennessee converged on Vancouver's station and besieged it. Suddenly Shawnee and Mingo, Cherokee and Choctaw saw in Vancouver more than a mere backwoods trader and they resolved that he and all other white intruders into the Valley of Mystery must go. Within a fortnight, Vacouver's party fled up the Tug and in the winter of 1790-1791 no white man built a fire anywhere in the hills west of Hollow Mountain and the Great Laurel Ridge. The Big Sandy, the easternmost valley in Kentucky, was the last to be settled. Of all the Dark and Bloody Ground, the Valley of Big Medicine was the last to be surrendered.

But when Harman's adherents returned in the spring they brought numerous new recruits. Their pack animals were laden with lead, powder, salt, axes, plows, seed corn, and extra rifles. Their new fort stood near the charred logs of the old and in the next forty-eight months many skirmishes were fought about its walls. The settlers who began clearing fields when they were not "forting" included the venerable Henry Skaggs and his brother James, Tice Harman, with flecks of gray mottling his yellow beard, his brother Daniel and his nephew Aquila, Absalom Lusk, Job Anderson, and others named Holbrook, Leek, and Horne.

In 1794 Anthony Wayne's army of regulars and backwoodsmen crushed the Northern Federation of Indian Nations in the momentous Battle of Fallen Timbers. There, where a hurricane had broken the trees and felled them like jackstraw, the grip of the red men on the northwest was broken forever. The forlorn Shawnee, long in flight from the warlike Iroquois, were dispersed anew.

In the same years, white power tightened around the Cherokee. The same unquenchable flow of settlers penetrated their lands, killed their game, and spelled their doom as an aborigine nation. In a remarkably short space of time they adopted the white man's ways, became literate and civilized, and inspired the admiration and respect of humane and thoughtful people everywhere. Forty years after Jenny's captivity the tribe was governed by a written constitution and exercised the disciplines and restraints of a democratic society. They flourished until a vindictive President and Congress defied an edict of the Supreme Court and expelled them onto the distant and sun-baked plains of Oklahoma.

But all that was unforeseen when Jenny came home again. Then the Shawnees were a mighty nation along the Ohio, and the Cherokee were a power to be reckoned with in the fastnesses of Tennessee.

In 1800 Jenny and Tom Wiley moved westward into the new Commonwealth of Kentucky. She had never doubted that it would happen. Tom was a settled man who loved his land, but gradually he came to have too many neighbors. Some of them, moving in with wagon loads of household "plunder," looked with longing at his fences, barns and cabins, and offered him gold and cattle for his acres. The lure of new land and the freedom to be found only "farther west" became irresistible and the farm he had wrested from the wilderness passed into the hands of a stranger.

In following the deepening trails to the west, they left behind few friends or kinsmen except the dead. The dust of Hezekiah Sellards had joined that of his son and grandchildren in the little flower-bordered graveyard on the hill overlooking the valley. John and Elizabeth Borders, John Sellards and many others had long since forsaken Walker's Creek. None ever returned, even for a day, and the ties of blood and friendship pulled those who lingered away, to pursue those who had already gone. So on a March day in the last year of the old century Tom and Jenny Wiley, their children, their dogs and their cattle made camp ten miles from the cliff on Little Mud Lick where Jenny had spent so much of her captivity. They found a winding valley that had never been touched by a settler's axe and Tom began clearing the bottoms of trees and wild cane. In time a new cabin of neat, hewed logs was raised and the farmer from the north of Ireland saw his name affixed to a little portion of the American land. The stream is called Tom's Creek to this day.

Tom and Jenny raised their second family there within visiting distance of their cousins, the Borders and Sellards children. The Skaggses moved on a bit farther, to the head of the Little Sandy. This land, too, filled with people. By 1802 most of the settlers passing through were headed for Ohio, and by the hundreds the children of the Kentuckians joined them.

Jenny's friend Tige had a place of honor and affection at their hearthside for many years and grew old as their children grew up. A joke had it that Jenny loved her dog "more than anybody else in the family." He died wrinkled and toothless after they moved to Kentucky and Jenny mourned his death as the passing of a loyal friend and comforter.

Tom Wiley died in 1810, esteemed for his integrity, courage and knowledge of the land. Jenny survived twenty-one years longer to the age of seventy-one. Even in old age she remained handsome, with hair that grayed slowly, and with immense strength and patience in her features. Her children, after the frontier fashion, married early and produced large families, so she had many grandchildren to mourn her. Her grave was dug beside her husband's and may still be found by patient searchers who rake away the leaves on a little point near the town of Paintsville—a name derived from the Painted Licks.

The legend of Jenny Wiley has set her name, too, upon the land. The great sycamore, where Dull Knife killed her baby, survived to 1850 and was called "Jenny's tree" by two generations of mountaineers. The little stream by which it stood was called—as it still is—Jenny's Creek. And beyond the Tug and Levisa in Kentucky is another stream—the one Jenny followed on that long-gone day when she obeyed the omen of the hopping bird. It, too, was given her name by settlers who had heard her story and Jenny's Creek still tumbles into Big Paint Lick, honoring to our own time the first white woman ever to wade its waters.

Today the descendants of Tom and Jenny Wiley, John and Elizabeth Borders, the Skaggs brothers and the Harmans are found over a broad mountain region and in many western states. When he grew old, Tice Harman returned to Virginia where a tiny hamlet still bears his name. The spirit with which he had mastered so much of the wilderness lived on in other borderers until, two generations after his death, they leaned upon their long rifles and gazed upon the Pacific.

Actually the adventures of Jenny Wiley were—and are—illustrative rather than remarkable. Similar hardships and horrors were visited upon countless frontier women during the long, epic struggle to clear the American land of its original and tenacious inhabitants. Between 1492 and 1892 more white people—men, women and children— perished at the hands of the Indians than were killed on all America's battlefields, at home and abroad, in all her other wars. Thus our land acquired its legends. Happily in the Kentucky mountains, the tradition of one woman's endurance has survived.

Many Shawnees died in the campaigns that ended at Fallen Timbers. A tradition relates that the cunning medicine man—some even called him a witch or sorcerer—died there. Dozens of scalps were brought back by triumphant Kentuckians but none claimed to carry the hair of Black Wolf, the slyest of Shawnees. For several years after the battle a small band of Shawnees prowled the Kentucky hills west of the Little Sandy, sometimes attacking isolated cabins or a flatboat drifting on the Ohio. They found lead somewhere in the mountains and knew how to compound their gunpowder from saltpeter, sulfur, and charcoal. They never numbered more than a half-dozen, and were never overtaken by the white militiamen who pursued them so often. Excellent trackers who could judge a man's height and weight and size and age by his tracks upon the snow thought one of them was slender and old. He may have been Black Wolf. And toward the end he may have led his tiny band out of the hills he knew so well and across the Ohio, Indiana and Illinois to those tribes still in arms against the whites.

Of the Cherokee Dull Knife, we can speculate with a little more assurance. Chief Benge made his last raid against the Virginia settlements in April, 1794. Coming down from Ohio with a mixed band of Shawnees and Cherokees, he attacked several cabins, killing, scalping, and burning. The countryside was quickly aroused and Lieutenant Vincent Hobbs pursued the marauders with a score of militiamen. They prepared an ambush in a deep, laurel-grown chasm at the base of a rock-strewn mountain with a roaring stream tumbling at its base. Benge and several of his followers fell before the first volley and the scalp of the notorious half-breed was prominently displayed and passed from hand to hand at the next muster day. But in dying, the warchief set his name upon the land. He was slain where a stream surges down the rocky slopes of High Knob—a wild, clear stream Virginians call Benge's Branch.

Another warrior who lost his scalp that day at Prince's Flat was a Cherokee—sturdy, with graying hair, thick cruel lips and a sullen expression even in death. Baubles of hammered silver decorated his limbs and clothing. When the scalp was torn from his head an old and deep scar marked his forehead. A wrinkled militiaman named Fraley, who had come into the country very early as a contemporary of the Harmans, looked at the corpse and said it looked like Captain John.

Another story has it that he died in Kentucky at the hands of an old and war-hardened adversary. James Skaggs related that in 1800 he was stalking a deer on the upper reaches of the Little Sandy. A movement caught his eye, and, cocking his rifle, he slunk behind a tree. A silent game of cat and mouse ensued, ending when a copper-colored face peeped from behind the silvery trunk of a huge beech. Skaggs was a deadly marksman and the ball struck the red man between the eyes. He was old and alone and carried nothing of value except a few pieces of hammered silver and a handsome rifle. Skaggs was certain he had killed Dull Knife. This Indian's scalp lock was probably the last taken in the Kentucky hills and the silver trinkets descended with the Skaggs name for several generations.

In any event, neither Shawnee nor Cherokee came after that to the long ridges of Western Virginia or to the low and close-set hills of Eastern Kentucky.

The land Jenny Wiley knew has been used with terrible savagery by industrial America. Generations of logging have reduced the vast and majestic forest to barrens and thickets and stands of trees unworth the cutting. The land has been torn and mutilated by strip-mined digging for the coal found in such abundance within the hills. Scores of burning slate dumps send a pall of polluted air to hang above the polluted streams winding now by rotting, half-abandoned coal towns. Discarded automobile hulks, heaps of trash and other modern obscenities rust and rot where herds of bison once grazed on young cane and wild grasses. But at dawn and sunset the land is still beautiful, still savage of aspect, as in the days when it was the West—a new nation's first and bloodiest frontier.

AFTERWORD

Author's Historical Afterword

The modern technological revolution that effectively insulates most Americans from want and hardship serves, also, to cut them off from much of their history. Moving frequently from job to job and city to city, millions have become virtually placeless—almost wholly bereft of the ties to land and people that gave continuity, strength and purpose to earlier generations.

As one glides effortlessly, and in air-conditioned comfort, across the nation, the landscape blurs and distances lose meaning. If one thinks of such matters at all it becomes practically impossible to measure mountains, valleys, swamps, and streams in the kind of terms that made sense to unmechanized man. Our machines cushion us against fatigue; food is chiefly a problem for the overfed, and except for brief intervals, surgery and drugs subdue pain. Even in warfare there is a measure of pity and a time of rest.

With all its distractions our era has brought unparalleled peace and security to most Americans. They hear no shot fired in anger; they sleep peacefully at night. It is easy for them to forget that it was not always so. For centuries our continent was a battleground in one of mankind's longest, cruelest, and bloodiest conflicts. The vacationers who traverse the land would do well to consider the names that spring at them from bridges and signposts. They tell, if one cares enough to inquire, tales of anguish, loss, despair, love, anger, hate, vengeance, bloodshed, birth, death, defeat, and victory. Medicine Bow, Defeated Creek, Bull Run, Indian Creek, Johnson's Fork, Buffalo Gap, Council Bluffs, George's Creek, Hungry Mother Mountain, Jake's Branch, French-man's Bend, Betty Troublesome Creek, Dead Man's Gulch—where but in the United States do such marvelous, such generous, provocative, manly appellations wait to greet and intrigue a traveler? They are the stuff of history, the elemental substance of our national story.

Each terrain feature was once part of the western horizon, looming ominously but irresistible before a race of people who moved always toward the sunset. They bled as they crept westward and often they moaned or shrieked in the grip of unspeakable misfortune. But they did not stop. Each river, ridge or plain once knew struggle and gave rise to stories that survived for several generations. Then, gripped by other interests, men forgot. But still the rough, spare names survive. Much of the American epic is preserved in them and in nothing else. Daily they whisper of old and unremembered enterprises to people who are too preoccupied to hear. This little book tells how some quite ordinary and otherwise undistinguished places acquired the names by which they are called to our own time. I hope they will never be known by others.

For one hundred and fifty years the frontier that began at Jamestown on Virginia's coast in 1607 had crept slowly westward. A tremendous amount of history had been crowded into those brief decades. An alien people from an alien clime had begun hesitantly with a tenuous hold on a bit of sandy shore. As they grew in numbers their impudence grew also, so that they unhesitatingly wrested from ancient Indian nations such lands as they could not buy. And the red men who had met the first of the newcomers with openhanded generosity and a childlike eagerness to trade for the white man's baubles learned too late that their ancient hunting lands could not be shared. The palefaces cut down the trees, built fences, and set small armies of glistening black slaves to plowing, planting, and hoeing corn and tobacco. Thus for a century and a half the line of settlements crept westward slightly more than a mile a year.

This westward-moving border between encroaching whites and bitterly resentful and warlike red savages was a crucible of fire and agony. It tempered men, women, and children to endure and achieve, to suffer and bleed and then return to the task of conquering a continent. Out of this crucible arose the western backwoods people—Americans with roots in many European countries but so tempered in arm and heart that their breed would reach Oregon, 2400 miles away, in only ninety more years.

Europeans, using elaborate Old World methods, could not subdue the American wilderness—a fact well demonstrated by the crushing defeat of General Edward Braddock's army at Fort Duquesne on July 9, 1755. Braddock's superbly trained regulars and ill-disciplined colonial militiamen were all but annihilated by leather-shirted Indians firing at them from a thicket. In the French and Indian War—the American phase of the vast war for empire between Great Britain and France—the French and the Indian allies strove to confine

English penetrations to the lands east of the Appalachians. Had they succeeded, the English-speaking United States of America might be today a long coastal shoestring, a North American Chile. But while they bled at Fort Duquesne and on countless lesser battlegrounds, the colonials were learning, and, as in so many things, they were learning from their foes. Before the frontier disappeared forever, the backwoodsmen would learn to live in the immense wilderness as easily as the Indians and to traverse it as tirelessly. But their relationship to their wilderness environment would never be an easy one, as it could never be a long one. The white borderers came to consume, to tame, to rule a wilderness the aborigines (indigenous inhabitants) sought only to inhabit.

But while the line crept inexorably toward the dark hills to westward, the two disparate worlds that collided with each other for the first time at Jamestown made subtle accommodations to one another. The red nations of hunter-warriors and corn-tending squaws became habituated to the white man's trade goods. Rifles, steel knives and hatchets, whiskey and rum, combs, mirrors, wool and cotton shirts and blankets, dyes, kettles, needles, thread, buttons, gunpowder and lead—these and many other items were eagerly embraced by a Native, less commercial people. To buy them, they were compelled to hunt relentlessly for the pelts coveted in the European markets. The wildlife that once abounded in all districts rapidly thinned and the hunters were driven to ever-longer forays into distant territories in order to accumulate the indispensable bales of skins. Thus the Indians became a commercial people, their old mores and traditions shattered, their morals increasingly debased and corrupted by their growing dependence on their avaricious adversaries.

And the process created dependence in Europe, too. Cheap furs and leather—pouring in by the shipload—clothed and decorated the masses and the classes alike. Huge profits built great fortunes and the royal treasuries were fattened by taxes levied on the trade. Too, the cost of supporting armies to defend settlements was a burden that the kings and their councils sought to avoid. Thus it came to pass since 1763 that King George III of Great Britain—with the approval of the Board of Trade and the tacit concurrence of his fellow monarchs in Madrid and Paris—solemnly proclaimed that his subjects would henceforward remain to the east of the crestline of the Appalachian Mountains. The line of demarcation extended from Canada to Spanish Florida. It would separate red men from white, preserve the domains of the hunters and assure a perpetual flow of furs and skins, soothe the Indians, and establish peace. Someday, of course, the line would be breached and English-style farms would spread to the distant Pacific, but in the meantime the Indians would have been civilized and Christianized, becoming loyal subjects of his Majesty's government.

The scheme was an excellent one and thoroughly logical. It would, it appeared, solve many thorny and persistent problems. For twenty-one years the proclamation was a basic part of Great Britain's policy in the New World.

The tribes were pleased with the scheme. The planters and farmers in the settled lands were delighted. Their tenants and the multitudes of indentured servants, whose labor supplemented that of their black chattels, had been constantly wandering off to the frontier to build cabins in ragged clearings and avoid the terms of their service. Lenders had seen their debtors disappear in the same frustrating manner. Truly, the proclamation would be a blessing.

But it did not work. The westward impetus had grown too strong, the frontier people too numerous to be checked in such manner. Despite courts-martial and summary executions, the borderers passed through the gaps into forbidden valleys. When the King's men hunted them down and burned their pathetic cabins, they built them again. Neither gallows nor the fear of Indian reprisals kept them within the bounds of the proclamation. And when the red men realized that the King and his redcoated soldiers could not stanch the flow of people into their lands their wrath and vengeance were terrible indeed.

Bands of men, women and children with a few bony cattle and many savage dogs pushed originally into the Shenandoah, then beyond to the Cow Pasture, the New, the Cheat, and the Monogahela rivers. Just before the Revolution they broke through the range into the plains of Central Kentucky. And to the long, bloody border wars that preceded the proclamation were added the thirty years of frightful struggle that ended with Fallen Timbers in 1794. The frontier bled and burned in a conflict of immeasurable grimness and tenacity.

Almost to a man (and woman) the settlers abhorred authority. To the overwhelming majority, government was synonymous with oppression. Most were descended from penniless and landless farmers or orphans left fatherless by Europe's endless wars. The same wars that spawned so many widows and orphans produced, also, contractors who grew rich providing munitions and material. These nouveaux riches acquired broad estates, dispossessing many smallholders. Even the landed gentry were bound by the laws of primogeniture and younger sons generally lacked a living in their native lands. Soldiers set adrift after their service ended were often without jobs or food. Dispossessed farmers, orphans, younger sons of landed squires, war veterans, and the victims of almost innumerable penal laws—all alike found themselves on ships headed for the American colonies. Then, too, there were dissenters of all sorts, religious and political, who sought the freedom to dissent by heading for the New World. Occasionally these unfortunates and dissidents were joined by an honest man of means who sought an opportunity to enhance his fortune in the colonies, and by rakehells hopeful of a chance at fame and easy wealth. In full measure these worthies and their descendants gravitated to the western border. There, after July 4, 1776, they saved the West for the new nation then aborning, but that is a long and important story in itself.

None of this border humanity entertained any sympathy for the copper-colored people who had lived on the continent since time immemorial. They held the Indian in contempt and scorned his claim to the land as a palpable absurdity. And, as a descendant of countless generations of proud and courageous warriors, the Indian hated the whites because of their contempt of him. He loathed the "palefaces" because they violated so many of his taboos and traditions. To the grave, dignified and solemn native, the invaders of his domain were boisterous, "white-eyed," hairy obscenities. In a contest joined on such grounds there could be no thought of quarter.

The white border population was a curious conglomerate ranging from newly arrived and practically helpless refugees to woodsmen as skilled and sensitive as the Indians themselves in the arts of wilderness warfare. In the years after the end of the Revolutionary War, the feeble government created by the framers of the Articles of Confederation was helpless to defend them and the backwoods people became supremely self-confident—at once farmers, hunters, explorers creeping ever westward from clearing to clearing, folk physicians, lawmakers, ministers and, always and everywhere, soldiers. And in all these activities, children, women, and men were joined together by a common and wholehearted impulse. In a stump-dotted "new ground" miles from the nearest neighbor, where painted and cruel warriors might lurk behind every tree and stone, there could be no place for any shirker.

The backwoods people were drawn, in the main, from Scotland, Ireland and England. Everywhere, however, these stepchildren of Great Britain were preceded by the French—cunning and elusive traders and trappers who traversed immense distances to barter with tribes whose hunting grounds were so remote that they were virtually unheard of in colonial capitals. Fewer in numbers, but supremely important, were the Germans whose forebears had been set adrift by the convulsions of the Thirty Years' War. Hardened to strife and privation by countless struggles in their homeland, they gravitated to the frontier and gave strong leadership, thrust, and tenacious purpose to the westward movement. Without these uprooted "Dutchmen" the frontier would have moved much more slowly. In fact, it may be argued that without them the proclamation would have succeeded.

The Appalachian frontier was advanced by clan settlements—each consisting of a half-dozen or so families who relied upon each other for defense and rescue and whose young intermarried to strengthen the ties of friendship with bonds of blood. Sometimes they were supported by rifle-carrying black slaves, many of whom deserted to join the red enemy. From time to time, the clan was weakened by the defection of a family returning eastward to safer lands or, more likely, spinning off by itself and pushing far ahead of the clan's blockhouse. These "tomahawk settlers" built their cabins on remote creeks away from tribal trails and in virtually total isolation came to be almost as wild as the creatures they hunted for meat and clothing.

The backwoodsmen threatened not only the aborigines but the European empires which laid pretentious claims to vast territories farther west. Baron Hector de Carondelet, Spanish governor of Louisiana, described them in terms that clearly showed his alarm:

> This prestigious and restless population, continually forcing the Indian nations backward and upon us, is attempting to get possession of all the vast continent which those nations are occupying between the Ohio and Mississippi Rivers and the Gulf of Mexico and the Appalachian Mountains. . . . Their method of spreading themselves and their policy are as much to be feared by Spain as are their arms. . . . Their wandering spirit and the ease with which those people procure their sustenance and shelter quickly for new settlements. A carbine and a little maize in a sack are enough for an American to wander about in the forests alone for a whole month. With his carbine he kills the wild cattle and deer for food and defends himself from the savages. The maize dampened serves him in lieu of bread. With some tree trunks crossed one above another, in the shape of a square, he raises a house, and even a fort

that is impregnable to the savages by crossing a story above the ground floor. The cold does not affright him. When a family tires of one location, it moves to another, and there settles with the same ease. . . . If such men succeed in occupying the shores of the Mississippi . . . nothing can prevent them from crossing . . . and penetrating into our provinces on the other side.

On the far-flung frontier men suffered horribly. More than a score of tribes—perhaps a hundred thousand people in all—contested every new penetration into the Appalachians and the plains beyond. From their villages in remote fastnesses the warriors struck relentlessly. No season, no day, no hour was without its stark peril. They were masters of stratagem, of mobility, moving like shadows through immense forests and striking forts and isolated cabins with surprising and ferocious audacity. The burning cabin, surrounded by dead and mutilated bodies and broken household furnishings, was long the border's prime symbol. And captives, usually children and women, multiplied in the Indian towns, for the warriors were a capricious lot who sometimes showed mercy even after the tomahawk was uplifted.

Thus it was in the hills of western Virginia when George Washington became the first President of an out-landish new republic in 1789.

EPILOGUE

The Writing of Dark Hills to Westward

During the more than four decades that I lived near the headwaters of the Kentucky river, Harry and I traveled, by foot and by car, through and over the maze of mountains that make up the central Appalachians. I came to have a soul-felt respect and awe of those magnificent forested slopes, and their lovely cool hollows and burbling clear streams. With Harry as guide and teacher, I came to understand something of their geology, their complex and delicate ecosystems, and their history. And I grieved with him at their destruction.

When he wrote the story of Jenny Wiley, it came from his love of that forest fastness and his identification with those early ones, both aboriginal and European, who had inhabited it. Dark Hills to Westward expresses his need to share and explain that heritage.

It was not until some years later that our pursuit of family histories and the reading of early frontier accounts discovered to me a far off grandmother, Theodosia Vause. With her two daughters, she was carried away by the Indians at the bloody massacre at Fort Vause, at present Shawesville, Virginia. A generation later, another of my ancestors, Jacob Spahr, was killed by Indians in an attack on Strodes Fort near Winchester, Kentucky.

On one of the trips we made to Frederick County, Virginia delving into our frontier origins, we identified the Old Zane's forge neighborhood, the site of an early Indian attack. A John Day testified that in his boyhood his mother's brother was there killed and she was abducted along with his two sisters. He was with the party who pursued the Indians. They found his mother dead, scalped, and naked in the woods, but went on to rescue his two sisters. We thought it probable that this was Harry's John Day ancestor though there is a confusion in the records as there was more than one "Indian fighting John Day" on the frontier. Another family tradition relates that Harry's great-great-grandfather Branson was scalped as an infant and left for dead, the only survivor of an Indian attack on his family's frontier home.

Thus the story of Jenny Wiley is but one tale in the long and bloody struggle in which our ancestors pushed the American frontier through the mountains of Appalachia, leaving an indelible stamp on our heritage.

About the Author

It was 1945. The war continued and I was soon to graduate from the University of Kentucky. Then I met Harry Monroe Caudill, just taking up his college career again, after being badly wounded in Italy and discharged from Army hospitals. Already he was outspoken and controversial. One of the first conversations we had was at lunch in the student center. I remember it vividly. He pointed to the huge photographs of Kentucky scenes decorating the walls and said, "Look, all tobacco and horses and agricultural scenes. There is nothing to indicate that Eastern Kentucky and its industrial powerhouse is a part of the state. The university ignores the eastern third of the counties." This was a new concept for me, as I had grown up in central Kentucky and, like most of my associates, was only dimly aware of the eastern coalfields myself. Then he went on to tell me of the poverty, and about the lack of roads, schools, health facilities, and jobs. And he told me of the government planning before the war to turn vast stretches of the Kentucky mountains into national forest lands as had already been done in Virginia and the Carolinas, moving people out to the cities to find industrial jobs. He believed there were other solutions. Here, I thought, was a man with ideas and vision, no longer a boy with idle interests and conversation. And so, not long after, I agreed to marry him, and when he finished law school we returned to his mountain homeland to build a home, a family, and a law practice.

Harry laughed. He relished the ridiculous and the absurd. He observed humanity and he chuckled. And he made us all laugh, for he was a master teller of tales about people, their foibles, their inconsistencies, their peculiar strengths. And he laughed with the children. As they rode to school each morning, he sang old songs, making up silly doggerel to fit the melodies as he drove along. Sometimes for days at a time nearly everything he said came out as amusing rhyming couplets, an expression of his joyous exuberance.

And he walked in the woods, determined to strengthen his shattered leg. He walked for hours on the soft forest loam, often alone, but glad of the company of family and friends. Across our pastures and through the little gate we entered into an almost endless woodland. Sometimes, on longer expeditions, we camped and hiked to beauty spots in the Pine Mountain woods, the Red River Gorge, or the Smoky Mountains, accompanied by friends, the children and their friends, pausing often to loiter on a fallen log and listen to Harry telling a tale of the olden days, or expounding on the magnificence and fragility of the landscape before us. This was our cherished and preferred entertainment. After the children grew up and left home, their friends remembered and sometimes came to talk with us by the fireside or on a shady summer porch.

Harry talked. His inquiring, cogitating, philosophical and restless mind expressed a constant flow of commentary, interspersed with humor, recollections, all in vivid language. His everyday speech was a unique combination of phrases from the King James Bible, Shakespeare, and the classics, mixed with mountain colloquialisms. He talked of growing up in the Depression years in the coalfields, and of his war experiences. Both had a deep and abiding effect on his life.

As an infantry soldier, he scrambled up the slippery rock-strewn, eroded slopes of the Italian mountains where he was eventually wounded and crippled for life. He was haunted by the remains of villages he saw there, abandoned generations before because the mountains had been completely denuded of their forest cover and then grazed to the bedrock. He saw how easily the same thing could happen in his own Kentucky mountains, a process indeed already begun. The experience fired his urgent insistence in later years that surface mining be controlled, a battle he waged for decades using every tactic he could summon.

We nourished our land from worn-out hillside cornfields into rich pastures, timberlands, lawns and gardens. We worked together growing and harvesting large gardens of marvelous vegetables to serve the table to which so many friends and sojourners were invited. For we were both farmers at heart.

Harry was outraged. As his law practice grew, his clients often were coal miners and their families, or those whose land had been damaged by mining operations. He observed how welfare became a permanent way of life for too many families because there was no industrial development beyond the coal industry. He saw more and more clearly how the region and its people were exploited, how their birthright had been sold for a mess of pottage. And he longed for the people to take charge of their own destiny, to build for themselves a vibrant and growing society in which the eastern part of Kentucky would come into full and equal partnership with the rest of the state.

The Kentucky legislature seemed the place to begin. He served three terms and his deep mountain voice was heard often and noted by the newspapers. Sometimes his statements were outrageous, but they caught public attention. He made people aware of those long-ignored eastern counties. His leadership in bringing about school consolidation, the severance tax on coal, reclamation of strip-mined lands, and other changes is a matter of record.

But to be elected and stay elected, one must compromise, and he found that telling all that needed to be told irritated many powerful interests who opposed him. Instead he turned to writing and speaking, utilizing media attention to focus public opinion across the state and bring pressure on the legislature.

As our children grew older, I felt the need to return to some kind of public life. Though the post of agricultural extension home demonstration agent was then vacant in our county, I decided not to return to the profession, choosing to work with my husband and fit my scheduled work into the needs of home and children. Soon I was a part of his busy law office staff, and as his writing career developed I devoted much time to helping with his manuscripts and the monumental correspondence he carried on outside his legal practice. Later, during the years when he was teaching at the University of Kentucky, I searched for Appalachian-related materials, which I copied for his research files.

Harry read. He read voluminously: history, biography, current affairs, always piecing together the pattern of cause and effect that had created a unique Kentucky society. And from a rocking chair in our kitchen he read aloud to me, or discussed what he had read, as I attended to the needs of children and household. This was his way, I think, of clarifying and fixing in his own mind what he read and observed. It made humdrum chores pass quickly, and for more than forty years I was educated by a born and gifted teacher.

Harry wrote about what he had heard, what he had witnessed, what he had read, and his readers understood. They understood how the mountain society came to be as it is, and to see some of the potential for desirable change. They responded in countless letters. They came from across the state and nation, and from foreign countries, to talk to him and to interview him for newspapers, magazines, and television. Bureaucrats, social workers, health workers, religious workers, university professors and their students, and volunteer workers came. Some remain friends to this day. Our lives were tremendously busy, sometimes exhausting, but never dull. The conversations around our dinner table were stimulating and varied, and often we had overnight guests whom we had never met before they arrived on our doorstep. Our eldest son was of an age and turn of mind to enjoy and take part in the discussions; our daughter, three years younger, accepted our busy household as a matter of course; the second son nine years younger recalled no other style of living.

Harry spoke. He spoke to all who would listen. As his reputation grew, he was petitioned more and more to speak in far-off places, and always he wanted me to fly or drive him. It would have been impossible without the always available loving attention of his parents, who lived not far away. With the assistance of ample household help, they often stayed with our children with such sincere pleasure that I felt free to help Harry.

In all of this he remained accessible to the many clients, present and past, of his law office. In a country practice it is necessary to be easily available to troubled clients who have little knowledge of the intricacies of the courts. Our telephone rang constantly, each call brought some new problem or a client needing reassurance. It was a heavy burden at times. I marvel still at his vitality. Through it all he was constantly writing or dictating. In the end he wore himself out.

He was disappointed, sometimes discouraged to the point of bitterness, that apathy and ignorance combined to obstruct needed change. Then again he was hopeful as he saw ignorance dissolving and efforts beginning to bear fruit here and there. His were large visions, practical ideas worth pursuing, worth the doing. I believe deeply that his life made a real difference, that his imprint is visible in the region he loved.

It was a wonderful life we shared for forty-four years. I count myself as truly blessed to have been a partner in all the undertakings of a unique, complex, and gifted statesman, a man of courage constant to the end.

Anne F. Caudill

The Jesse Stuart Foundation

Incorporated in 1979 for public, charitable, and educational purposes, the Jesse Stuart Foundation is devoted to preserving the legacy of Jesse Stuart, W-Hollow, and the Appalachian way of life. The Foundation, which controls the rights to Stuart's published and unpublished literary works, is currently reprinting many of his best out-of-print books, along with other books which focus on Kentucky and Appalachia.

With control of Jesse Stuart's literary estate—including all papers, manuscripts, and memorabilia—the Foundation promotes a number of cultural and educational programs. It encourages the study of Jesse Stuart's works, and of related material, especially the history, culture, and literature of the Appalachian region.

Our primary purpose is to produce books which supplement the educational system at all levels. We have now produced more than thirty editions and we have hundreds of other regional materials in stock. We want to make these materials accessible to teachers and librarians, as well as general readers. We also promote Stuart's legacy through video tapes, dramas, and presentations for school and civic groups.

Stuart taught and lectured extensively. His teaching experience ranged from the one-room schoolhouses of his youth in eastern Kentucky to the American University in Cairo, Egypt, and embraced years of service as school superintendent, high-school teacher, and high-school principal. "First, last, always," said Jesse Stuart, "I am a teacher. Good teaching is forever and the teacher is immortal."

In keeping with Stuarts devotion to teaching, the Jesse Stuart Foundation is publishing materials that are appropriate for school use. For example, the foundation has reprinted seven of Stuart's junior books (for grades 3-6), and a Teacher's Guide to assist with their classroom use. The Foundation has also published several books that would be appropriate for grades 6-12: Stuart's Hie to the Hunters, Thomas D Clark's Simon Kenton, Kentucky Scout, and Billy C. Clark's A Long Row to Hoe. Other recent JSF publications range from books for adult literacy students to high school and college texts.

Jesse Stuart's books are a guideline to the solid values of America's past. With good humor and brilliant storytelling, Stuart praises the Appalachian people whose quiet lives were captured forever in his wonderful novels and stories. In Jesse's books, readers will find people who value hard work, who love their families, their land, and their country; who believe in education, honesty, thrift, and compassion— people who play by the rules.

Books By Harry M. Caudill

Night Comes to the Cumberlands, 1963.

Dark Hills to Westward: The Saga of Jenny Wiley, 1969.

My Land Is Dying, 1971.

The Watches of the Night, 1976.

A Darkness at Dawn, 1976.

The Mountain, the Miner and the Lord, and Other Tales from a Country Law Office, 1980

Theirs Be the Power: The Moguls of Eastern Kentucky, 1983.

Lester's Progress, 1986.

Slender Is the Thread: Tales from a Country Law Office, 1987.